THERE WERE SCREAMS,
AND THEN THERE WERE *SCREAMS*.

Alex hurried to the sound of the scream. It was coming from the unfinished shell of the new main Keeper's Quarters. Though there was a ball of fear gnawing at his gut, Alex hoped it was just another snake sighting, but somehow he knew this time that it was more than that.

Alex saw Rachel Seabock as he neared the shell of the structure, but his gaze was only on her for a second. Someone had skewered Jefferson Lee through the heart with a shaft of cold, black iron, pinning him carefully to the thick pine timber of the new building . . .

The blacksmith had put on his last exhibition.

Don't miss the first Lighthouse Inn Mystery:

Nominated for the Agatha Award:
Best First Novel

Innkeeping with Murder

". . . Should be just the beginning of a long stay."
—*Ft. Lauderdale Sun-Sentinel*

Lighthouse Inn Mysteries by Tim Myers

INNKEEPING WITH MURDER
RESERVATIONS FOR MURDER

Reservations for
MURDER

Tim Myers

BERKLEY PRIME CRIME, NEW YORK

RESERVATIONS FOR MURDER

A Berkley Prime Crime Book / published by arrangement with the author

PRINTING HISTORY
Berkley Prime Crime mass-market edition / June 2002

Visit our website at
www.penguinputnam.com

ISBN: 0-425-18525-7

Berkley Prime Crime Books are published
by The Berkley Publishing Group,
a division of Penguin Putnam Inc.,
375 Hudson Street, New York, New York 10014.
The name BERKLEY PRIME CRIME and
the BERKLEY PRIME CRIME design
are trademarks belonging to Penguin Putnam Inc.

PRINTED IN THE UNITED STATES OF AMERICA

10 9 8 7 6 5 4 3 2 1

For Patty and Emily,
the two women in my life who make it all worthwhile

Acknowledgments

I'd like to thank the following people for their contributions to this book, and more importantly, to my life.

Kim Waltemyer, my wonderful and gifted editor, for plucking me out of the slush pile and changing my life forever.

Tamar Myers and the late Liz Squire, for their friendship, laughter and encouragement.

Corki, Jan, Carolyn, Hannah, Cindy, Ed, Sarah and all the staff at the Hickory Public Library, my true friends in books.

Tracy, Linda, Danny, Rich, GeeGee, Mary, John, Karen, Tom, Lelia, Maryelizabeth and all the other booksellers across the country, for taking me into their hearts.

Ruby Hall and Bob Myers, my parents, for their love and support.

Jim, Wayne, Randy, Tom, Bob and Paul, true brothers in my heart.

Kathy, Jay, Amy, Paul, Sarah, Tom, Charlotte, Patrick, Katy, Mary, Steve, Bernadette, Matthew, Veronica, Bill, Theresa, Monica and Martha, the best family I could have ever married into.

For those, now gone but never forgotten, who were such an important part of my life, and the very best parts of me: Chris Myers, Dorothea Hurley, George Hurley, Katherine and Lawrence Pickering.

And as always, for Patty and Emily. I couldn't have done it without you.

1

"Alex, we need to talk."

Alex Winston looked up from the pile of bills he'd been wading through to find The Hatteras West Inn's housekeeper, Elise Danton, standing by his desk. He'd seen that determined look in her eyes before. "Can it wait, Elise? I really need to go through these bills this morning." Though they'd uncovered a handful of gems a few months earlier on the property, there hadn't been enough from the sale to do everything Alex wanted to with Hatteras West. Emma Sturbridge, his resident gem expert, hadn't yet been able to locate the vein where they'd originated, and Alex was beginning to wonder if she ever would.

Most of the money from the sale of the emeralds had gone into the reconstruction of the Main Keeper's Quarters, a building that had burned to the ground earlier. Alex's inn was a near replica of the Cape Hatteras Lighthouse and its outer buildings, with one major exception. Instead of being close to the ocean, his lighthouse was deep in the foothills of the North Carolina mountains.

And Alex was determined to return the place to all its former glory.

"Alex," Elise said, "you know you can do those later. I've already taken care of the urgent ones. We've got an inn full of people, and the fair starts in two hours." She frowned slightly. "That's what I need to talk to you about."

Alex said firmly, "Elise, I know you're not happy, but I'm not going back on my word. I made a promise to Shantara Robinson that she could tie her Golden Days Fair in with the Lighthouse Lighting, and I won't disappoint her. I'm sorry." The Lighthouse Lighting was the annual county-approved testing of the tower's beacon. People gathered from seven counties to see it, and it had always been one of the high points of Alex's tenure as the innkeeper at The Hatteras West Inn.

"Alex, we agreed that in order to stay in business, we need to start attracting a wealthier clientele. The fair defeats that entirely."

"But Shantara was desperate when Lucius Crane reneged on his offer to use his farm for the fair. There was no place else she could hold it on such short notice."

Elise paced around the room. "I know how much friendship means to you, Alex, but you've got to think of your inn first. I shouldn't have to remind you how close you came to losing Hatteras West before."

Alex shook his head. "Believe me, I know that better than anyone. Don't worry. The fair will tie in perfectly with our lighting ceremony. I wouldn't be surprised if we attract more guests because of it." He added softly, "Elise, everything's going to be fine."

At that moment, there was a scream just outside Alex's office.

Alex and Elise bolted out the front door together to find Marilynn Baxter, one of the exhibiting potters, pale and quivering on the front porch.

"What's wrong?" Alex asked, searching for some reason, any reason for the woman to have screamed so fiercely.

"I saw a snake," she said shakily, her finger pointing to the small copse of trees that stood between the inn and Bear Rocks, a granite formation close to the inn that sported the oddest shapes and forms in twelve counties.

"It's all right now," Elise said, scanning the ground near them. "Whatever it was is long gone."

Craig Monroe, the other half of the husband-and-wife pottery team participating in the fair, came rushing up to them. "What happened, Marilynn? I heard you scream! Are you all right?"

Suddenly conscious of all of the attention, Marilynn said curtly, "I saw a snake, Craig, a big one."

"It was probably just a garter snake," Alex said, trying to ease some of the tension.

"It doesn't matter what kind it was," Marilynn snapped. "I hate all snakes! They are absolutely vile creatures!"

Craig put an arm around his wife. "You're okay now. Let's go finish setting up, Marilynn. There aren't any snakes around our exhibit."

"There'd better not be," Marilynn hissed as her husband led her back to the temporary fairground. Craig Monroe offered a silent shrug of apology to Alex as they walked away.

As Alex and Elise started back inside, she paused and said good-naturedly, "If I can't get you to change your mind about this fair, we should at least see what we've let ourselves in for. Are you interested in walking around the displays before Shantara opens the gates? Things were so crazy last night, I didn't even have a chance to see them setting up their booths."

Though Alex knew Elise wasn't thrilled about having the Golden Days Fair at Hatteras West, he realized that she would never let anyone else know how she truly felt. The offer of a tour was her concession to making the best of what she considered a bad situation.

"Sounds good to me," Alex agreed as they reversed directions.

The two of them gave the pottery area a wide berth as they started their tour.

Bill Yadkin, one of the two blacksmiths working the fair, already had a hearty fire going in his portable forge. The big, fierce-looking young man stared intently at the coals as they burned. Rachel Seabock, a traditional woodworker who used only the hand tools she'd inherited from her great-grandfather, hovered near the young blacksmith. Though Rachel was a decade older than Bill, it was obvious from the look in her eyes that there was more than just friendship between the blacksmith and the woodworker.

Alex thought about skipping past them, but Elise forged on before he could steer her to another exhibit. She said, "That fire feels good this morning," as she warmed her hands near the coals.

Yadkin smiled. "We'll see how you feel around noon when the day starts to heat up."

"No thanks," Elise said. "What's in the fire?" she asked, pointing to the center of the forge. Alex looked into the burning coals and saw a foot-long tapered shaft of metal glowing a dull orange.

"I'm making another stake for Rachel's canopy. Somebody walked off with the last one."

Rachel said proudly, "Bill's building up quite a clientele. His business is really taking off."

"You don't have to sell me every minute of the day, Rachel," Yadkin said shortly.

"I wasn't . . . I didn't mean . . ." Rachel said, looking flustered. After a deep breath, she continued. "I'd better take Jenny that rocking chair she ordered before the fair gets into gear today," Rachel said. "I swear, I never thought a weaver would be one of my best customers," she added with a shrug before hurrying off.

After she was gone, Alex said, "Rachel's a big fan of yours, isn't she?"

Yadkin shrugged. "Yeah, too much, sometimes," he grumbled as he moved the glowing shaft around with a long set of tongs.

As Yadkin started to pull the steel from the fire, he warned, "You'd better move."

Alex and Elise took a few steps back as the young blacksmith pulled the glowing rod from the fire. In a practiced motion, he began pounding the steel with a scarred and worn hammer on the broad, flat top of his anvil. The anvil seemed to sing with each strike, and in moments the shaft's tip was tapered to a point. Yadkin studied it a moment, then plunged the steel back into the fire for another heat.

"That's fascinating," Elise said after he was done. "It's like alchemy."

"I guess," Yadkin said with a shrug.

Alex asked, "How did you learn to do that?"

"My dad had his own forge when I was growing up. It was a hobby for him, but it's the only thing I know how to do." The young blacksmith was a great deal more eloquent with his hands than with his words.

Alex looked at some of the pieces on the display table in front of the blacksmith's booth. "That's an interesting swoop," he said as he fingered a delicate curlicue on the end of a fireplace shovel.

"It's my trademark," Bill said heatedly, "no matter what Jefferson Lee says. I hear he's been making pieces using it just to spite me!"

"You don't get along with the other blacksmith?" Alex asked gently.

"He's not a blacksmith," Yadkin said with a snort of derision. "He's a showboat and a bully, but he's not a blacksmith. Not in my book, anyway."

Yadkin's tongs dove back into the fire as he pulled the tapered shaft out again. He laid the metal across a wedge protruding from the top of his anvil, and with a quick strike, he separated the spike from the body of the iron. Another flurry of strikes, and the butt end was bent at a ninety-degree angle. After a rapid dunk in the bucket of water beside his forge, the spike was done. It was beautiful, even with its simple form and function.

"I've got to get this to Rachel," he said, dismissing them in an instant.

As Alex and Elise moved on, she whispered, "He's an interesting fellow, isn't he?"

"Rachel seems to think so," Alex answered. "You know, I never would have put those two together."

"Love has a mind of its own sometimes," she said as they approached the next exhibition spot.

Jenny Harris, an attractive blonde in her early thirties, was working at her loom, weaving an intricate pattern of yarns into what looked like a shawl. As she worked, a clamor of bracelets and necklaces tinkled like wind chimes. Jenny obviously made all of her own clothes, using material laced with splashes of colors and designs unique to her work. Alex noticed that

Jenny's feet worked the pedals of the loom in a constantly shifting yet graceful dance as she shot a threaded block back and forth across the top. She stopped the second she saw them approach.

"Hi Alex, it's so good to see you again," Jenny said as she abandoned the loom for a moment and stood.

Alex explained, "Things have been crazy at the inn lately." Elise coughed gently beside him.

He added, "Jenny, this is Elise Danton. Elise, I'd like you to meet Jenny Harris. She's an old friend."

Jenny laughed. "I was a great deal more than that not so long ago." Jenny gave Elise her brightest smile as she said, "Pleased to meet you."

Elise said, "I've got to admit, I've always been fascinated by weaving. Could you give me a quick lesson?"

Jenny said, "Absolutely, I'd be delighted."

As Jenny sat back down on her portable bench at the loom, she pointed to different parts of the setup as she explained, "This is the reed. These are harnesses and heddles. See the threads of yarn going through?" She held up the wooden spool. "This is called a shuttle. It rides back and forth like so. The foot pedals control the raising and lowering of the warp, that's these long strands of yarn here, and the shuttle bobbin carries yarn across for the weft." As she slid the shuttle back and forth in easy, practiced motions, the shafts rose and fell in a graceful dance at the touch of her foot pressure. As Jenny pulled the main frame back to her, she said, "The beater comes back to snug things up, and you're ready for another row."

Elise nodded. "Wow, it seems really complicated."

Jenny smiled and said, "It's not as hard as it looks. It's like most things; you get the hang of it after you do it long enough."

Elise jogged Alex's elbow as she said, "Thank you for the lesson. It was nice meeting you, Jenny."

"Thanks for stopping by. Don't let Alex work you too hard. I've heard he can be hard on his maids."

Elise was more than just the maid at The Hatteras West Inn; she was actually better qualified to run the inn than Alex was, but she just smiled and nodded in response.

Alex said, "She's the one keeping me busy," and he turned to go.

"Don't be a stranger, Alex," Jenny said as he and Elise walked away.

Alex was glad to see Jenny in such a chipper mood. They'd only gone out a handful of times before their relationship lost its steam. Sandra Beckett, an attorney in town, had been his main on-again-off-again girlfriend for much of the past couple of years, but he'd ended their relationship soon after Elise came to Hatteras West. It had startled him to discover that Sandra was much nicer as a friend than she'd ever been as a girlfriend. Unfortunately, the one woman Alex was interested in dating was his "maid"—and she was engaged to someone else.

Shantara Robinson hurried up to them and grabbed Alex's arm. "Alex, have you seen Jefferson Lee? He should be getting ready for the fair, but I can't find him anywhere."

As Elise moved back toward the inn, she said, "If you two will excuse me, I've got rooms to clean." She added softly, "Good luck, Shantara."

"Thanks," she said as Elise departed. When the maid was gone, Shantara said, "Alex, I like that woman."

"It's been a godsend having her at Hatteras West," Alex agreed.

Shantara looked over at the empty blacksmith's

space and said plaintively, "Where could Jefferson be, Alex? It's just like him to disappear right before we open the gates."

"Take it easy, Shantara, we'll find him. At least you've got one blacksmith here and working."

Shantara frowned. "As much as I like Bill Yadkin, Jefferson Lee's the real draw. I can't run my fair without him."

Alex said, "Don't worry, he'll turn up. Are you managing to enjoy any of this? You did a great job putting the fair together."

Shantara smiled. "I'll enjoy it more after it's over. Right now, all I want to do is survive the experience. Alex, I really appreciate you letting me move everything out here at the last minute."

"Hey, what are friends for? Now, let's go find your wayward blacksmith," Alex said. "I'm sure he's around here somewhere."

As they started their search, there was another scream a thousand yards away.

It was getting to be a trend Alex could learn to live without.

2

"What's going on," Shantara asked breathlessly.

"I don't know," Alex answered as he hurried toward the sound of the scream. It was coming from the unfinished shell of the new Main Keeper's Quarters. Though there was a ball of fear growing in his gut, Alex hoped it was just another snake sighting, but somehow he knew this time it was more than that.

There were screams, and then there were *screams*.

Alex saw Rachel Seabock trembling as he neared the shell of the structure, but his gaze was only on her for a second.

Someone had skewered Jefferson Lee through the chest with a shaft of cold, black iron, staking him to the thick pine timber of the new building like a butterfly on a pin.

"Oh, no," Shantara gasped as she ran up beside Alex. "This is horrible."

Alex touched her arm gently. "You don't need to see this. Why don't you take Rachel back to the inn."

It took Alex and Shantara a full minute to get Rachel to go with them. She was obviously still in shock, deathly silent after her piercing scream.

Shantara said softly, "I can't believe someone killed Jefferson Lee." With a quaver in her voice, she added, "I hate to do this, but I don't have any choice, Alex; I've got to cancel the fair."

He knew that Shantara had staked everything she had on the success of the Golden Days Fair, mortgaging her country store in the hopes of a big payoff.

Alex said, "Don't do anything rash, Shantara. Let me call Sheriff Armstrong. If we're lucky, he won't have to shut you down."

As the three of them walked toward the inn, Alex called out to Bill Yadkin. The young blacksmith joined them, looking uncomfortably at Rachel. For once she didn't even seem to notice him standing there.

Alex said, "I need you to stand guard over the new building. Someone's killed Jefferson Lee, and I don't want anybody messing around with the evidence until Sheriff Armstrong gets here."

Was it Alex's imagination, or did Yadkin look unsurprised by the news of Jefferson's death?

He didn't have time to think about it at the moment, but the blacksmith's expression unsettled him.

Alex found Sheriff Armstrong at the first place he phoned. The sheriff loved Buck's Grill more than just about any place on Earth. Alex often found him there, parked on the stool by the door, greeting customers and campaigning in his never-ending battle to get reelected.

Alex cut through the small talk that started just about every conversation in Elkton Falls. "We've got a body out at Hatteras West, Sheriff."

"Murder?" the sheriff asked.

"I'm afraid there's no doubt about it this time," Alex acknowledged.

"I'll be right there," Armstrong said. "No sirens this time, Alex. I promise."

The sheriff had won his last reelection by the narrowest of margins over the town barber, and Alex had found him a changed man. Gone was the blustery posturing and the officious manner, replaced by a constant effort to always do better, knowing that he was serving by the skin of his teeth.

"Hurry," Alex said as he hung up the phone.

"Alex?"

He hadn't even heard Elise behind him.

She asked, "Did I hear you right? Has someone been murdered?"

Alex nodded glumly. "Somebody killed Jefferson Lee at the construction site."

"Oh, no."

"We'll get through this," Alex said. "I'd better get out there and help Bill Yadkin make sure no one disturbs the crime scene."

"There's no doubt in your mind it was murder?" she asked, a thread of hope lingering in her voice.

"Sorry, there's no doubt at all," Alex said. "Somebody pinned him to one of the posts with a steel shaft."

"I'm coming with you," she said doggedly.

Alex paused a moment, then said, "Thanks for the offer, but I need you at the front desk, Elise." His real motivation was sparing her from seeing the body. There was no need for her to share the nightmares he'd be having when he finally closed his eyes.

He was surprised by how readily she agreed.

As Alex made his way across the grounds to the new building, he couldn't help wondering why murder had come back to Hatteras West. He looked up at the light-house beacon, a constant presence that he never took for granted.

Surely the sentinel had seen the crime and the killer as well.

If only the lighthouse could talk.

Bill Yadkin didn't have anything to say as he and Alex waited for the sheriff, though Alex tried to draw him out several times. The oddest thing was that the young blacksmith kept his back to the body, while it seemed that everyone else was closing in for a better look at the last remains of Jefferson Lee.

As good as his word, Sheriff Armstrong showed up on the scene less than fifteen minutes later, his siren silent all the way.

Armstrong, his uniform bulging from his girth, asked as he looked up at the lighthouse, "Am I going to have to climb those infernal steps again?" Irene Wilkins, the sheriff's cousin who acted as the town beautician and resident crime-scene expert, got out of the other side of the patrol car with her investigation kit tucked under one arm.

Alex said, "No climbing this time. It happened in the middle of my new construction. Sorry to drag you out here, Irene."

The older woman shrugged. "It's not a problem, Alex. I don't have a perm scheduled until eleven, so I'm free till then."

Armstrong said, "Let's go see what happened."

Alex led them to the building site. Nearly all of the exhibitors and guests at the inn had gathered near the new construction to get a look.

Armstrong said in a mighty voice, "Nothing to see

here, folks. Move along so we can begin our investigation."

The group broke up reluctantly, and Armstrong nodded to Irene. "Why don't you go ahead and get started."

She already had her camera out and was taking pictures of the body and the area around it.

Yadkin came up to Alex and said, "If you don't need me anymore, I've got to bank my fire. I guess this means we're shutting down."

"You bet your hat it does, son," Armstrong said.

Alex said, "Let's not be hasty, Sheriff. Technically, this area isn't even a part of the fair."

"Now Alex, I've got a responsibility to the town to solve this murder. It's gonna have to take priority over Shantara's fair."

Alex said, "Sheriff, there's got to be a way to keep the fair open. You know as well as I do how much Shantara has riding on this."

Armstrong bristled. "It can't be helped, Alex. I'm not about to let a thousand people walk around the crime scene. We have to secure the area."

Alex called out to the beautician, "Irene? How much time do you need before you release the area?"

She lowered her camera, looked around the construction site for a good thirty seconds, then said, "Give me an hour, tops. I'll need help getting that steel out of him after I dust it for prints, not that it's going to do any good. The metal's rough and unpolished; I doubt I'll get a thing from it. If we call the wagon now to come get him, we'll have this part of it wrapped up well before the fair starts."

Armstrong cut off Alex's next words before he even had the chance to speak. "I'm not having it, do you hear me? This is too important, Alex."

Alex said evenly, "Sheriff, look at it this way. If you shut the fair down, you're going to lose most of your suspects. You can't just keep them here all weekend without some kind of justification. But if you keep the fair going, you'll know where every one of them is. That way, you can interview them at your own pace. You can cordon off the building site if you want, just in case. Keeping this fair alive has got to be the best alternative for everybody involved."

Armstrong seemed to think about it for a full minute before he looked at Irene and said, "Are you sure you'll be done in time? I don't want you rushing on account of the fair."

"I said I'd be done in plenty of time, didn't I? Believe me, in an hour there won't be anything else to learn at this crime scene." Irene was rightfully smug about her abilities. She'd recently won a state competition for the thoroughness of her work, something that had galled many of the full-time investigators who'd competed for the prize.

Armstrong seemed to take forever to finally make up his mind, but ultimately he nodded his agreement. "Okay, but I'm going to need a few conditions. I want to post one man right here to watch over the scene during the fair. Agreed?"

"Fine by me." Alex didn't really want a deputy standing around, but if it would make the sheriff happy to have one of his men on site, it was little enough to deal with.

Armstrong said, "The other thing is, I'll need a room to interview my suspects in."

"Sheriff, every room I've got is booked right now. There's not an empty spot in the inn."

"Then I'm just going to have to—"

Alex cut the sheriff off, knowing what was coming next. "But you can have my office. Will that do?"

"I guess it will have to," Armstrong said grudgingly. The sheriff knew firsthand how small Alex's office was.

"Thanks, Sheriff," Alex said, slapping Armstrong on the back. "You're doing the right thing."

"I just hope I don't regret it later."

Alex nodded his agreement. He'd never say it out loud, but he found himself hoping for the very same thing.

Shantara and Elise met him at the door before he even had the chance to get inside the inn.

"What did he say?" Shantara asked, the resignation heavy in her voice. "He's shutting me down, isn't he?"

"The fair can go on," Alex reported.

It took a moment for his words to sink in.

Shantara said haltingly, "I can't believe it. What did you say to him?"

"I just pointed out that if he shut you down, he'd lose most of his suspects. Shantara, it won't do anybody any good if the fair's canceled. Armstrong could see that."

Shantara said, "Alex, I don't know how I can ever thank you."

"Just go out there and make it a success."

"Aren't you two coming?" Shantara asked as she headed for the door.

"We'll try to come out later, but we've still got an inn to run."

"And I've still got my fair!"

After Shantara was gone, Elise said, "Alex, I don't know how you did it, but you saved the day."

"All Armstrong needed was to see things objectively."

Elise said, "Now that you've taken care of that, what are we going to do about this murder?"

"We're going to let Sheriff Armstrong handle it," Alex said firmly.

From the look in Elise's eyes, Alex could see that she didn't believe him, not for one second.

3

Alex tried to clean off the pile of papers on top of his desk before the sheriff started his interviews. He was still working when Armstrong came to the door with Shantara not far behind. Evidently, she was first on the sheriff's list of suspects, something that surprised Alex.

"Let me just get this out of the way," he said as he opened the top drawer of his desk and shoved the rest of the bills inside.

Alex was about to leave when Shantara asked, "Alex, is there any way you could stay for this?"

Armstrong said, "Now, Ms. Robinson, this is just a preliminary interview. Having Alex here isn't going to do you any good; he's not a lawyer."

"No, but he's a friend, and I can use all of those I can get right now."

Alex said, "Shantara, I don't know what I can do, but if the sheriff doesn't mind, I'd be glad to stay. But honestly, maybe you'd *better* call a lawyer."

"I don't need one, not if you're here with me."

Put that way, Sheriff Armstrong had little choice but to let Alex stay. They'd worked together often enough in the past, albeit reluctantly at times.

Alex felt strange seeing Sheriff Armstrong sitting behind his desk, Shantara across from him. There was no room for a third chair in the small space, so Alex leaned against the rich, honeyed pine wall.

The sheriff pulled out a small notebook and said, "First of all, where were you last night?"

Shantara looked surprised by the question. "I was home asleep. Where were you?"

Armstrong frowned. "Now, Ms. Robinson, you won't do yourself any good by having an attitude with me."

Alex said, "Sheriff, where else would you expect her to be? And why should it matter where she was last night?"

"My investigator just informed me that the time of death was most likely sometime between midnight and four A.M." The sheriff added, "Alex, I've agreed to let you sit in, but you're going to have to keep your comments and questions to yourself if you want to stay."

"Sorry," Alex said contritely. He didn't believe for one second that Shantara was guilty of murdering Jefferson Lee. She had too much to lose, even granting the wildly remote possibility that anything could push her to such a desperate act.

Armstrong nodded once, then said, "Ms. Robinson, can anyone verify that you were home last night?"

Shantara said, "Are you asking me if I'm sleeping with anybody at the moment, Sheriff?"

Armstrong blustered, "Now, ordinarily, that would be none of my business. I don't much care what grown, consenting folks do behind closed doors, but I'm trying to see if you've got any kind of alibi for the murder."

Shantara shook her head. "I'm sorry to say that I sleep alone these days, Sheriff."

Armstrong pushed on. "Did you make any calls or get any during those hours? Can anybody verify you were home?"

"I turned off the ringer on my phone and put the answering machine on last night. I was whipped from moving the fair yesterday at the last minute, and to be honest with you, I'd just about had my share of people for the day."

Armstrong wrote something else in his notebook, then said, "Okay, let's move on. Did you have any reason to kill Jefferson Lee?"

Alex had a tough time keeping his mouth shut. The very nature of the crime most likely cleared Shantara in his mind. He doubted she'd have the physical strength to skewer the blacksmith, even if she *had* motive enough to do it.

Shantara said calmly, "I knew him, but I had no reason to want him dead. Even if I *were* going to kill him, why would I do it at my own fair? I've got everything riding on this, Sheriff."

That was a point Alex had wondered about himself.

Armstrong said evenly, "Maybe you weren't thinking clearly. He goaded you into a rage, and you killed him. If it was self-defense, I'm sure we can work something out."

"I work out at Tracy's Gym sometimes, but I'm not that strong." Shantara turned to Alex. "You saw how he was pinned to that post. Do you think I could possibly do that?"

Remembering Armstrong's warning, Alex merely shook his head.

"Alex, I warned you—"

Shantara interrupted. "He didn't say a word, just like you told him."

Armstrong studied Alex a second, then turned back to Shantara. "Have you ever seen the metal rod that was used to kill Jefferson Lee?"

"I've seen a dozen of them, Sheriff."

"Where?" Armstrong asked as he sat up abruptly in the chair.

Shantara said reluctantly, "If I don't tell you, I'm sure somebody else will. That shaft had Bill Yadkin's swooping curlicue on the end. It's one of his. There's no doubt about it."

It was amazing how fast the sheriff wrapped up the rest of his interview with Shantara. As Armstrong hurried out the door, he said, "You're free to go for now, Ms. Robinson, but don't leave town."

After the sheriff rushed out, Shantara said wearily, "I hate sending him after Bill Yadkin, but he was bound to find out sooner or later."

"It's not your fault, Shantara." Alex had recognized the distinctive pattern on the shaft as well, but he'd refrained from telling Armstrong about it until he had a chance to talk more with the young blacksmith himself. Knowing Yadkin's gruff nature, it would be all too easy for the sheriff to take his responses as hostility, and Armstrong did not respond well to attitude from anyone.

In less than two minutes, Armstrong was towing the young blacksmith into Alex's office.

"I need some privacy for this interview," Armstrong said. "You're both going to have to clear out."

Alex tried to protect Yadkin as best he could. "Do

you want me to get you a lawyer?" he asked before the door could close. Alex's former girlfriend Sandra Beckett was the only lawyer in Elkton Falls he knew well enough to call, but he didn't want the young blacksmith intimidated into saying something he shouldn't.

Yadkin snapped, "I've got nothing to hide. I hated the snake, and everybody knows it."

Armstrong's eyes lit up as he pushed Alex and Shantara out of the office.

"This is not good," Shantara said plaintively. "What are we going to do?"

There was only one real choice in Alex's mind.

He had to call Sandra, whether Yadkin wanted her or not.

Sandra's secretary put him through immediately. The lawyer said, "What's up, Alex? I'm buried under a mountain of paperwork at the moment."

Alex said, "I wouldn't bother you if it weren't important. Bill Yadkin's in trouble. Sheriff Armstrong is interviewing him right now about the murder of Jefferson Lee, and I'm afraid he's going to say something he shouldn't."

Sandra shifted gears quickly. "I heard about the murder a few minutes ago." It always amazed Alex how fast news traveled in the small town on the kudzu vine, faster than any gossip's grapevine in the world.

Sandra asked pointedly, "Why does the sheriff think he's guilty?"

"A shaft of iron with Yadkin's trademark on it was used to kill Lee, and I just heard Yadkin tell the sheriff that he hated the man's guts."

"Don't let him say another word, Alex. I'll be out there in seven minutes."

Rachel burst into the inn as Alex was hanging up the telephone. "Where are they? I just heard the sheriff hauled Bill away."

"Take it easy, Rachel. They're in my office. I just spoke with Sandra. She's agreed to talk to your boyfriend, but he's refusing his right to a lawyer."

"We'll just see about that," Rachel said as she pounded on Alex's office door.

As the door opened, Rachel tried to push past Armstrong, but the sheriff wouldn't budge.

Nearly out of breath, Rachel said, "Sheriff, you can't talk to him without his lawyer present."

"I offered; he declined. Besides, no charges have been filed. Now, you're interrupting an official investigation here."

Rachel shouted, "Bill, don't say a word. Alex called a lawyer for you."

"I don't need a lawyer. I didn't kill him," Yadkin snapped.

Rachel said fiercely, "You idiot, that's why you need someone to protect you."

Yadkin said strongly, "I can handle this myself, Rachel. I don't need you meddling."

Instead of backing down this time, Rachel said firmly, "If you do this on your own, we're through! I mean it, Bill. You of all people should know I don't make idle threats."

Alex wondered how much effect the ultimatum would have on the young man. Finally, just as the sheriff smiled at the silence, the blacksmith said, "Okay, you win. I guess we'd better wait for this lawyer fella."

"It's a woman, and she'll be here any minute," Rachel explained, the relief thick in her voice.

Armstrong looked like he was ready to spit nails. "Alex, I want to talk to you. Now!" He pulled Alex by the arm into the lobby, away from everyone else. "Now, why did you go and do that? He was almost ready to confess!"

"Sheriff, how can you be so sure he did it? I was afraid he'd say something to you he couldn't take back."

"That's why I was pushing him!"

Alex matched his tone. "And that's why I called Sandra!"

"Listen up, Alex, I'm not going to put up with you sticking your nose in this case, you hear me?" Armstrong took a deep breath, then said in an easier tone, "I'm the first one to admit you've helped me a time or two in the past, but that doesn't give you the right to interfere. Do I make myself clear?"

Alex nodded. "I hear what you're saying, but you can't expect me to stand by and just watch, can you?"

"You'd better believe it," Armstrong said. "Now, I'll thank you to stick to running your inn, and I'll handle the investigations around here."

4

Alex watched as the sheriff stormed back into the office. He was probably right. Investigating crime was a job for the sheriff, not for an innkeeper. But there was no way Alex could just stand around and watch the young blacksmith hang himself!

Armstrong suddenly bulled out of Alex's office with Bill Yadkin in tow.

"Out of the way, Alex," the sheriff said as he led the young blacksmith to the door.

"Where are you taking him, Sheriff Armstrong?" Rachel demanded. "You can't arrest him until his lawyer gets here."

"Tell Sandra we'll be over at the jail. I'm finishing this interview downtown, where there will be less interruptions." He looked pointedly at Alex as he said the last.

Rachel blocked their way. "You're not taking him anywhere until Sandra arrives."

Armstrong said, "Rachel Seabock, I've known you

most of my life, but don't you believe for one second that I won't arrest you for obstructing justice if you don't back off, and I mean right now."

Rachel was sobered by the thought of going to jail, but she wasn't about to give up. "I'm going with you then," she said resolutely.

"You can follow me into town, but you can't have a ride. I'm sorry, Rachel, but it has to be that way."

She pointedly ignored the sheriff and said, "Bill, don't say a word until your attorney gets there."

It looked like the young man was finally beginning to realize just how precarious a position he was in. Alex couldn't really blame Armstrong for his enthusiasm in going after Bill. After all, the young blacksmith had the means to commit the murder as well as a pretty strong motive. As to opportunity, Alex had to admit that just about anyone staying at The Hatteras West Inn could have killed Jefferson Lee. In Alex's mind, the most damaging piece of evidence was the metal spear used to stab the blacksmith; there was little doubt that Bill Yadkin had forged the skewer used to kill Jefferson Lee.

After Armstrong had taken Bill Yadkin away, with Rachel close on their heels, Alex looked around the suddenly deserted inn. The place was eerily quiet. Alex stepped outside for some fresh air. Springtime in the foothills of the Blue Ridge Mountains could be delightful, but it could also be a fickle friend. He'd seen it balmy and warm one day, only to have violent ice storms the next. Fortunately, for the fair's sake, the weather looked like it would be cooperating over the next two days.

On the wide, expansive porch at the front of the inn, Alex stood beside the half-dozen rocking chairs and surveyed the grounds. People were just beginning to file in, and with the murder on the grounds, it could easily turn out to be a record crowd. Shantara had had the foresight to sell daily tickets to the event, and from the number of people already drifting in, she'd easily earn her investment in the fair back today, leaving the next day for pure profit. His gaze automatically took in the new construction site, where one of Armstrong's deputies now stood guard.

Alex suddenly felt a meaty paw slap him on the back. "You just can't stay out of trouble, can you?"

Alex smiled brightly at Mor Pendleton. "You can't blame this one on me," Alex said as he looked at his friend. He and Alex had played football together, though Mor had been the star, while Alex had played more of a supporting role. A bad hit in college had wiped out Mor's knees, and the man had been forced to drop out of college and come back to Elkton Falls to join Lester Williamson in the handyman business. The two men were vital to keeping Hatteras West up and running, and Mor or Les was a welcome fixture to all of Elkton Falls.

"Where's Emma?" Alex asked lightly. His resident gem expert and his best friend had become quite an item around Elkton Falls lately.

Mor shrugged. "She's around here somewhere. That woman can surely be exasperating."

Alex laughed. "I've heard her say the exact same thing about you."

"I'll just bet you have," Mor said.

As Emma Sturbridge joined them on the porch, she said, "My ears were burning fiercely. Were you gentlemen by any chance talking about me?" Emma was a large, attractive woman with a sharp gleam in her eyes and a confident tone in her voice.

"What did you buy?" Mor asked, looking at the bundle under her arm and ignoring her question completely.

"I found the most delightful sweater. That Jenny can really weave, can't she?" Emma took her new acquisition out of the bag and held it up in front of her. The sweater sported a bright splash of colors that seemed to melt together in a most unusual pattern, but it suited her. Emma Sturbridge had come to the inn as a guest searching for some of the emeralds the area was famous for, and she'd ended up staying in Elkton Falls. The town had that effect on some people, drawing them in like bees to fresh blossoms. Emma now owned a crisply kept little cottage in town, and Alex believed that its proximity to Mor or Les's repair shop was anything but an accident. She'd been delighted to announce to Mor that she fancied him, and to Alex's surprise, it hadn't taken Mor long to reciprocate.

Mor said, "Emma, I've got to get back to town. I have a full schedule today." He laughed at Alex. "Believe it or not, you're not even on my list."

"The new boiler's running as calm and quiet as a whisper," Alex said.

Mor nodded. "I'm glad you took some of the money from the new construction budget to replace it, but I kind of miss hanging around, Alex." The old boiler had been a nightmare for both men, and Alex wondered which of them had been more relieved to see it go. It now resided, in various pieces, at Amy Lang's studio, destined to be wed with other discards to become another piece of her modern sculpture. Amy was fairly new to Elkton Falls, though her people had come from the Foothills several generations before. Once the fair was over, Alex promised himself to make it a point to visit her studio. After all, she was one of his closest neighbors, though their respective businesses kept them busy at their own tasks.

"Are you heading back with me?" Mor asked.

Emma said, "I think I'll stay and catch up with Elise. I haven't seen her in days. I'll see you tonight." She kissed Mor soundly, and he laughed brightly when Emma stepped back.

"You're good for me, woman," he said, still smiling.

"It's nice to be appreciated, but you're going to be late."

Mor grinned at Alex. "She's a worse slave driver than Les is."

"Oh, go on with you," Emma said.

After Mor was gone, Emma said, "Where's Elise? I want to show her my new sweater."

"She's somewhere inside," Alex said.

Emma patted his shoulder. "I'm so sorry about the murder. It's not your fault, Alex. You know that, don't you?"

Alex smiled sadly. "In my heart I know you're right. I'm sorry he's dead, but I realize this kind of thing happens all the time. I just wish it hadn't happened here."

As he watched more people stream into the fair, Alex saw Sandra's BMW cut through the crowd and make its way to the front steps of the inn.

She got out of the car, showing a flash of her long legs as she did. Sandra always wore the shortest skirts she could get away with in court. There was no doubt she got the male jurors' attention that way, but she held it with her persuasive arguments. When the two of them had been dating, Alex had sat in on one of her closing statements just to see her in action, and he'd been overwhelmed by her presence in court. Sandra was remarkably good at what she did, and Alex began to realize that she had won most of their arguments for a reason. That had been one of their problems. Sandra could convince him of just about anything when they were together. Only afterward did he realize that he'd been played expertly to come to the conclusions she'd wanted him to reach.

"Alex, it's good to be back at Hatteras West. I've missed this place."

Alex said, "I'm afraid you're too late, Sandra. The sheriff's already taken Bill into town."

"He hasn't arrested him, has he?"

Alex said, "No, but he said to tell you that he was taking Bill to jail so he could interrogate him without being interrupted."

"We'll just see about that," Sandra said.

Alex added, "Sandra, I'm not sure how he's set financially. I probably shouldn't have brought you in on this, but I didn't know who else to call."

She touched his arm lightly. "Don't worry about it, Alex. You did the right thing. I can always write it off as my contribution to the arts."

"One thing, Sandra. Bill Yadkin's got a real temper. It's not going to be easy representing him."

Sandra offered a smile. "Well, you know me, Alex. I always did like a challenge."

As she drove away, Alex wondered if he'd sent her on an impossible mission.

He had to admit that there was a very real chance Bill Yadkin had done exactly what it appeared, that the young blacksmith had killed off his main competition.

5

Alex knew it was pointless wading through the bills he'd thrown in his desk drawer. Just the thought of re-organizing them again was enough to kill the desire to work. His mind was on other things.

Murder had come back to The Hatteras West Inn, and it was a most unwelcome guest.

Alex decided that more than anything else, he needed some time on Bear Rocks. Slipping away to the top of the lighthouse gave him perspective on his problems when he needed a place to think, but touching the sun-warmed boulders always offered an overwhelming comfort he couldn't explain. The formation of weathered boulders, eroded into passageways, slides and bridges, had always had a calming influence on him. As a boy, Alex had memorized every twist and turn to the paths, and he prided himself on the fact that he knew the rocks better than anyone alive.

Cutting through the crowds at the fair, Alex ducked into the trees and soon found himself mostly away from the noise of their presence. He curled up into a cradle of warm stone and stared up at the sky. He hadn't been there long before a voice called out to him.

"I thought I saw you slipping away through the trees," Alex heard.

He looked up to find Shantara Robinson standing at the base of his rock.

Alex said, "To tell you the truth, I needed to get away from the world for a few minutes."

"I can relate to that," she said as she deftly climbed up beside him.

"Shouldn't you be at the fair?"

She shook her head. "I had to catch my breath, too. We've got a huge crowd, that's for sure. Only I don't think they came to see the artisans at work; they're more interested in seeing the crime scene. People can be such ghouls.

"So why are *you* up here hiding from the world?" She paused a second, then added, "As if I have to even ask. Alex, I'm so sorry I brought all this onto you and your place."

"Listen to me, Shantara, it's not your fault any more than it is mine. I just hate that it had to happen at all."

"Me, too, Alex." There were a few moments of shared silence, then Shantara stood up and brushed her slacks off. "Why don't we head back to the fair? People are probably wondering where we slipped off to."

Alex joined her as she deftly jumped off the rocks. He said, "Let them wonder. It will give them something to talk about besides the murder."

As they walked through the trees on the path that led back to the inn, Shantara asked soberly, "Alex, do you think Bill actually killed Jefferson Lee?"

"Well, he had motive enough. I've heard Jefferson was trying to drive him out of business by stealing all

of his customers. I don't have to tell you about Yadkin's temper, either."

"So you think he did it?" Shantara asked.

Alex took a few steps, then stopped as he said, "No,
I don't think he killed the man, but I could be wrong. I
couldn't tell you why, it's just something in my gut."

Shantara said, "So, if Bill Yadkin didn't kill him,
who did?"

"I wish I knew," Alex admitted. "Give Armstrong a
chance, Shantara. He'll uncover the truth."

"Not without you helping him, Alex. Everybody in
town knows how much he leans on you."

Alex held up his hands. "Shantara, I'm staying out
of this. I'm just an innkeeper, remember?"

"You're a lot more than that," Shantara said as she
stepped closer. "Alex, you can't just let this drop."
There was a catch in her voice as she added, "Don't
you understand? This is all my fault."

"You're not responsible for Jefferson Lee's murder,
Shantara."

"I just wish that were true," Shantara said, tears
creeping from her velvety brown eyes.

"Let it go, Shantara."

She shook her head. "I wish I could." Shantara took
a deep breath, then let it out slowly before she added,
"Alex, how long have we been friends?"

Alex said softly, "Since kindergarten. You used to
steal my sleep mat during naptime."

"That was the only way I could get your attention.
Alex, in all the years we've known each other, how
many times have I asked you for a favor?"

He started to answer when Shantara continued, "I
mean besides having the fair here at Hatteras West."

"Never," Alex admitted.

Shantara looked gravely into his eyes, then said,

"Well, they're coming in a flood, because this is going to be the second thing I've ever asked you to do for me. Alex, you've got to find out who really killed Jefferson Lee. The only thing is, you can't ask why it's so important to me. Just believe me when I tell you it is, more than you'll ever know."

Alex protested, "I'm not a cop, Shantara, I'm not even some fancy private detective. What makes you think I can find out who killed Jefferson Lee?"

"You were always good with puzzles, Alex, and you've got a way of making people talk to you. You really listen! Do you know how rare that is in this world? Will you do this, Alex? For me?"

"I don't know what I can do," Alex said, then added quickly, "but I'll try my best. For you."

Shantara gave Alex one of her rare hugs, then released him just as quickly as she'd embraced him.

Despite his best intentions to stay out of the murder investigation, Alex suddenly found himself right back in the middle of things.

And he still didn't have a clue why Shantara was convinced that Jefferson Lee's murder had anything to do with her.

Shantara had persuaded Alex to let her exhibitors stay at the inn during the two days of the fair at a greatly reduced rate long before the festivities had moved to Hatteras West's grounds. Elise hadn't even been able to disagree, since it was an extremely slow time for them anyway, and it did manage to fill up the rooms. The only room they had reserved for the weekend was #7, where Evans Graile was staying while his house was being renovated. Evans was an agreeable old man with a sharp eye and a soft voice; he never missed a thing and wasn't reticent at all about sharing his newfound information. Most days, he watched the outside world in one of the lobby's comfortable chairs from early morning till late into the night, and honestly, Alex had grown accustomed to his presence, but he'd been noticeably absent over the past few hours. Alex wondered where in the world the man could be.

Jefferson Lee had demanded the inn's nicest suite for himself, but Alex had refused to move Evans from his room. Jefferson had insisted that he was the fair's biggest draw, and Alex realized ironically that he'd turned out to be just that.

A thought suddenly occurred to him. Maybe there was something in Jefferson's room that would give Alex a handle on who had killed him. It was time to honor his word to Shantara and see if he could uncover who had murdered Jefferson Lee.

Alex felt like a ghoul and a burglar creeping into the room of the dead man. He knew the sheriff wouldn't approve of his snooping, even though Alex could probably justify his presence in some capacity as the innkeeper.

Jefferson Lee was as neat in private as the image he showed the world. His clothes were carefully folded in the Shaker-style dresser Alex's grandfather had built, and his toilet articles in the bathroom were arranged in an orderly fashion on the countertop. It was almost as if Jefferson had known he was going to die and hadn't wanted anyone to judge him by the condition of his room. Alex had once had an aunt who always cleaned her house meticulously before going on vacation, just in case something happened to her while she was trav-

eling. The irony was that she'd died when she slipped
in the tub while cleaning it just before going on safari.

Alex was just about to open the writing desk drawer
when the door behind him flew open. He felt his heart
hammer in his chest until he saw Elise standing in the
doorway.

"I thought I'd find you here."

"Come in and shut the door," Alex whispered
fiercely. "I don't want anybody to know I'm in here."

Elise stepped inside and closed the door behind her.
In a gentle voice, she said, "I thought you were staying
out of this."

"I promised Shantara I'd dig around a little," Alex
explained.

"Why is she so concerned about Jefferson Lee's
murder?"

"She feels responsible," Alex said as he opened the
drawer.

There were a few of the standard room postcards
with The Hatteras West Inn on them, the beacon shining out into the Foothills night. Alex was about to shut
the drawer when he noticed that one of the postcards
had writing on it.

He carefully pulled the card out of the drawer by its
edges and read the note printed in block letters nearly
pressed through the paper: "MEET ME AT NEW
BUILDING SITE TONIGHT. URGENT."

With a sudden sinking feeling in the pit of his stomach, Alex realized that he was probably holding the
lure that had been used to lead Jefferson Lee to his
death.

"Alex, you shouldn't have touched that; it's evidence," Elise said.

"I was careful, I picked it up by its edges. Elise, you
always put fresh postcards in the rooms, don't you?"

"Every day, without fail. That card was meant for Jefferson Lee. Alex, you know you can't keep it. It's evidence."

Alex started to slip it back into the drawer, then decided to leave it out in the open, just to be certain Armstrong would see it. "I'm not about to take it. I'm not sure it will do anybody any good; block lettering is almost impossible to trace. Anybody could have gotten the postcard; the inn's full of them. I've even got a ton of them in the lobby and in town for people to take."

"At least we know the murder was premeditated," Elise said softly.

Alex answered, "I'm not sure Armstrong's going to see it that way. To him, this could mean anything. It could have been about a lover's rendezvous or even an appointment for a business meeting."

Elise shook her head. "I don't think so, and you don't, either. Why would somebody print in block letters if their intent was innocent?"

"Hey, I agree with you. I think the killer wrote it, too." He studied the card another moment, then said, "You know, I'd really like a copy of this. Do you think I'd be risking too much taking it downstairs and making a photocopy?"

"Alex, I wouldn't try it," Elise said gravely.

"It might come in handy," he said stubbornly, pulling out his handkerchief and picking the card up carefully by the edges. "I'll have it back here before anyone knows it was ever gone."

Elise looked doubtful, but Alex was determined not to let the clue, or at least a copy of it, get away from him.

As they hurried down the stairs to the office, Craig Monroe, one of the potters, met them halfway up.

Monroe said, "We need some old towels if you've

got them. Somebody's walked off with some of ours, if you can believe it."

Alex hid the postcard behind his back as Elise said, "Why don't you come with me to the storage closet, and I'll see what we've got."

As Elise slipped past Alex, their eyes met for an instant. The warning in her glance was clear.

Alex carefully closed the door to his office and made three copies of the note, blowing one up to twice its normal size, just in case there was something he'd missed. The first copy he made was skewed, with part of the "URGENT" cut off, and Alex chucked it into the trash can after adjusting the card properly on the copier glass.

He had a horrible time finally getting the card off the glass of the copier without smudging any fingerprints that might be there, but it finally lifted off.

Alex's foot was on the top stair when he noticed that the door to Jefferson Lee's room was standing ajar. He knew he'd locked it carefully behind him a few minutes before.

It looked like Alex wasn't the only one conducting an investigation.

6

Alex nearly dropped the postcard when he saw Sheriff Armstrong standing at Jefferson Lee's writing desk, Elise a step behind him.

He tried to slip the card back onto the dresser when Armstrong swung around.

"What the devil's going on here, Alex?" the sheriff asked.

"What are you talking about?" Alex replied, slipping the card behind his back before the sheriff had a chance to spot it.

"You know full well what I'm talking about." Armstrong glared silently at him, and for a moment, Alex almost started to bring the postcard from behind his back when the sheriff continued, "I can't believe you put that she-dog on my tail, Alex. I thought we were friends."

"We are," Alex said.

"Well, you have a strange way of showing it," Armstrong said. "Sandra Beckett is the toughest bulldog in the pen."

"Bill Yadkin had to have somebody watching out for him, Sheriff. You know that as well as I do."

Armstrong replied, "Does it have to be Sandra? That woman is one purely vile thorn in my tail." He turned to Elise and said, "Pardon me for my language, Elise."

She smiled broadly at him. "Don't hold back on my account."

Alex said, "If you two will excuse me, I've got an inn to run." Now what was he going to do with that blasted postcard?

Elise saw that Alex was in a dilemma about the evidence he was concealing. She moved to the window and said, "Sheriff, what's going on out there?"

Armstrong joined her there, and Alex made his move. In less than two seconds, he had the postcard back into the drawer and had joined them at the window.

Armstrong blustered, "I don't see anything," as he looked out at the mass of people milling around the fair.

"I must have been mistaken. I thought I saw somebody fighting in the crowd. I guess I'm a little jumpy, with the murder and all."

The sheriff patted her shoulder. "Elise, it's perfectly understandable." He turned back to the desk and said, "Now, if you'll excuse me, I've got to get back to work."

"Where's Irene? Shouldn't she be dusting for prints?" Alex asked.

"She's up to her hips in some woman's perm. Who knows how long that can take. Irene promised me she'd be out directly. In the meantime, I'm having a look around on my own."

Armstrong took out his handkerchief and opened the desk drawer. "What have we here?" he asked as he studied the card Alex had just replaced, holding it carefully by its edges.

Alex looked over his shoulder. "It looks like a note to Jefferson Lee," he said.

"Now, Alex, there you go jumping to conclusions again. How do you know Jefferson didn't write this himself? He could have been planning a little late-night rendezvous and never got a chance to deliver it."

Elise said, "But if that's true, how did whoever he was meeting know to show up?"

Armstrong said, "There's all kinds of ways. Jefferson could have changed his mind about doing it in writing and told the killer face-to-face. Heck, he could have called him up on the phone."

"But you agree it's an important clue," Elise said.

Armstrong nodded. "You bet I do. I'll have Irene check it for fingerprints as soon as she gets here. You know, it could still help, even if it's been wiped clean. When I catch whoever killed Jefferson Lee, this could prove it was premeditated." Armstrong added, "I thought you two had an inn to run. I need to finish this in peace."

Alex left reluctantly, with Elise close behind. Once they were out in the hallway, Elise said, "I still can't believe Jefferson wrote that note himself."

"Fingerprints should prove it one way or another," Alex said.

"And if there aren't any?"

Alex said, "Then we're no worse off than we were before."

Alex was relieved to find Evans Graile downstairs, nursing a tall glass of iced tea. He had to admit that a part of him had been afraid to go in search of the man, nervous about what he might find.

One thing was certain; Evans was positively addicted to his own personal brew of tea. Before he'd been willing to relocate to the inn during his home's renovation, he'd insisted on two things: around-the-clock access to the stove and a portable refrigerator to store his tea in for nighttime. Evans was of the old school when it came to making iced tea. He wasn't interested in microwaves, solar energy, or any other process used to heat the water besides an old-fashioned copper kettle purring away on the range top.

"Alex, care for a glass of tea? It's going to be a brutal day out later."

Alex wondered why the man cared. He had barely moved one foot outside of the inn since he'd arrived.

Alex almost brushed the older man off. He had too much to do to stop and chat. But, he reminded himself, he surely wasn't in the innkeeping business for the money. It was the vast array of people who passed through his door that kept Alex enthused about Hatteras West.

"Maybe just a short one," Alex said as he took a rocker beside the older man.

"Why, that's delightful," Evans said as he reached into the cooler that was always beside him. He pulled out a chilled glass, carefully transferred a few pristine ice cubes into it, then poured Alex a liberal portion of steaming tea from his thermos into the glass.

Alex could hear the ice crack as he took the glass. "That's the key," Evans said solemnly. "The tea must remain hot until the last possible moment. When that rich steaming liquid meets the ice, ah, ambrosia."

Alex took a sip and had to admit it was the best iced

tea he'd ever had. It should be, after all the work the man put into his brew.

"Is this ConTea?" Alex asked, trying to hide his smile as he mentioned the brand name.

Evans looked so offended he nearly fell off his chair. "My good sir, I would *never* use a store-bought blend. Why, I have my tea carefully selected from only the finest . . ." His words trailed off as he saw the grin on Alex's face. Evans chuckled softly. "You're joshing me, of course. Alex, you're a bigger rascal than your father was, if that's possible."

Alex's father had run the inn before him, and while his dad had joked constantly with his guests and the people from town, his humor was usually in smaller supply with Alex.

Alex took a sip of tea, then said, "Thanks, I take that as a compliment. So, what do you think of our little fair?"

"It's quite exciting, what with the murder and all. I feel I'm right in the midst of it all here." In a pleased voice, Evans added triumphantly, "Alex, I believe I know who skewered the blacksmith."

That certainly got Alex's attention. "Did you see something, Evans? You need to tell Sheriff Armstrong; he's getting ready to arrest Bill Yadkin!"

Evans took a sip of tea, then said softly, "Easy, my boy. I have no direct evidence, but I've seen the world from this chair these last few days when no one has realized I've been watching. You'd be amazed by what I've witnessed."

Alex's hopes for a solution suddenly deflated. The murder was obviously just a puzzle for the older man to mull over during his massive blocks of spare time.

"So who's your chief suspect?" Alex asked.

"I'd have to say the sheriff is right this time, Alex.

Young Yadkin and Mr. Lee had a terrible squabble right in front of the inn yesterday as they set up their booths. Their tempers were boiling, I tell you."

"I don't know, Evans. I just can't see Bill Yadkin doing it, but you could be right."

Evans tapped his glass with a fingernail. "Of course, everyone else saw that argument, too. It could just be a clever ruse to frame young Yadkin. The murderer used one of his pieces to commit the atrocity, didn't he?"

Alex said, "I'm surprised you've already heard about that."

Evans laughed. "Alex Winston, you've lived in Elkton Falls your entire life. I thought you'd be used to the kudzu vine by now. Word spreads faster than the vine itself in summertime," Evans said as he took another sip from his glass.

Alex finished off the last of his tea and handed the glass back to Evans. "Thanks for the drink. It was excellent, as always."

"Are you certain you won't have another sip? There's plenty, Alex."

"I'd love to, but I've got work to do."

Evans shook his head slowly. "The harried life of the innkeeper, Alex, leaves little time for reflection."

Alex patted the man's shoulder gently as he stood. "You're preaching to the choir, Evans, but the work has to be done."

Alex went back to his office to retrieve the copies he'd made of the note he'd found in Jefferson Lee's room.

With a sinking feeling in the pit of his stomach, Alex realized the copies were gone!

Alex knew he'd left them on his desk by the copier in his rush to return the postcard to Jefferson's room. Why hadn't he tucked them safely away before he'd gone to return the original? It would have only taken a second or two.

Someone had to have real brass to slip into his office and take the copies. That meant that whoever had done it had most likely spotted Alex going into Jefferson Lee's room earlier.

Someone at the inn was watching him, and Alex didn't like it one bit.

Alex was just about to look for Elise when he suddenly realized something. He'd ruined the first copy he'd made, and he'd tossed the skewed sheet into the trash can beside the copier. Alex hurried to the trash and saw that the thief had missed one copy after all. The block letters, at least most of them, were printed firmly on the discarded sheet.

Alex smiled grimly to himself. He still had a copy of the note after all, one the killer didn't realize he had.

Now how in the world was he going to figure out who had written it? Alex folded the paper carefully in half and walked out to rejoin Evans Graile.

"Evans, did you happen to see anybody going into my office in the last twenty minutes?"

"Why, is something missing?" the older man asked eagerly.

Alex shook his head. "No, I just wanted to know if anybody was looking for me."

"Not that I saw, Alex, but I must admit I was busily brewing my tea until just a few moments before you joined me."

"Thanks, anyway," Alex said as he moved over to the front desk. He spun the guest book around and studied the names of everyone who had signed in recently to see if he could spot any similarities to the handwriting on the note in his hands. A slight chill swept over him when he saw Jefferson Lee's name written in flowing script. Could the man have printed the letter himself? Alex just couldn't bring himself to believe that. As he studied the sign-in book, it was impossible to match the block print on his copy with any of the guests' signatures.

He was just about to give up when a voice nearby caught him by surprise.

"What are you doing, Alex?"

7

"It's just one of my lists," Alex said as he quickly tucked the folded copy under his arm. "Running an inn, you have to keep lists of all kinds of things to do. Jenny, shouldn't you be at the fair?" When he saw the expression on her face, he added, "Is something wrong?"

Jenny admitted, "I just can't believe Jefferson's gone. It's finally hitting home. I just had to get away for a few minutes."

"I've heard you two were close." He watched her carefully for some kind of reaction.

Jenny frowned, her nose crinkling just like he remembered. She said, "That's not what I mean. Life is truly short, isn't it? Jefferson and I went out once or twice, but do you want to know the truth, Alex? I never really got over you." She moved a step closer, and Alex found himself backing into the registration desk.

"I seem to recall you were awfully glad to get rid of me at the time."

She wasn't about to let him off that easily. "I was a fool, Alex, and I'm not afraid to admit it."

Alex couldn't believe what he was hearing. "How come you never said a word about all this when I went back to Sandra? That didn't seem to bother you at all."

Jenny looked him straight in the eye. "It took me this long to realize just how wrong I was," she said strongly.

"Jenny, I'm truly sorry, but I just can't," Alex said, just as Elise walked up with a suitcase in her hand.

She said, "Alex, I'm sorry to interrupt, but we need to talk."

Alex said quickly, "You're not interrupting, Elise. We were just discussing Jefferson's murder."

Alex couldn't take his gaze off her bag. Was she leaving?

Jenny looked at Alex intently. "Well, I'd better get back to my booth before Shantara comes hunting for me. She doesn't want us taking any unscheduled breaks." She added softly, "Alex, we'll talk more later."

"I'm sorry, but there's nothing left to discuss," he said as she walked away.

Alex turned to Elise, gestured to the suitcase and said, "Don't tell me you're leaving."

Fighting back her tears, Elise said, "I just got a call from Peter. It's about Dad."

Alex knew how much Elise worshiped her father, an innkeeper himself, in the mountains of West Virginia.

"What happened?" Alex asked.

"Dad had a heart attack," she choked out. "They're going to do a bypass tomorrow. Alex, I hate to leave you like this, but I *have* to be there with him. Peter said it was imperative that I get there as soon as possible. I'm sorry, I have to go."

Alex said, "Absolutely. Let me grab my truck keys, and I'll take you to the airport."

"I talked to Emma after I got the call. She's going to drive me to the airport. You need to stay here with your guests, especially with this fair going on. I'm so sorry about this, Alex."

He touched her shoulder gently. "Hey, you need to be there for him. Don't worry about me. I'll be fine."

The inn's front door opened, and Emma hurried in. "Elise, I don't mean to rush you, but we'd better get moving if you're going to make that flight."

Alex nodded, then said, "Call me when you get there."

"Be careful," Elise said softly. "I'm not even going to ask you not to look into this murder while I'm gone."

He smiled. "Good, because I'd hate to have to lie to you."

"Elise, don't worry about Alex. Mor and I will keep an eye on him," Emma said.

After they walked out, Alex saw that Evans Graile had shifted his attention to him. The older man offered a gentle shrug before turning back to the window.

Alex couldn't believe Elise was really gone. He'd come to rely on her help in running Hatteras West, and if he was being strictly honest with himself, her company meant more and more to him every day.

There was no doubt that she had to go; her father needed her. And now that Elise was gone, Alex was going to have to work harder than ever.

But he wasn't about to give up his murder investigation. Alex had given Shantara his word, and it wasn't something he was willing to break.

• • •

"Alex, can I talk to you a second?"

"Shantara, I'm really busy right now. I'm up to my eyebrows in work."

"Please, it's important," she said.

Alex nodded reluctantly, then noticed that Evans Graile was listening to them, though his eyes were still focused outside. He was certainly getting a show for his money today.

"Why don't we go into my office," Alex said.

She followed him, and after they were inside, Alex asked, "So, what's going on?"

"I owe you an explanation."

"You don't owe me anything. I already said I'd help you."

"I wasn't playing fair with you before, Alex. I shouldn't have pressured you into this without giving you all the facts." Shantara let out an explosion of breath, then said, "I owed Jefferson Lee quite a bit of money. If the police investigation takes too long, I'm afraid it's all going to come out and make me look like I had something to do with his murder."

"How much are we talking about here?" Alex asked softly.

"Ten thousand dollars. It's enough of a motive to make me a suspect, isn't it?"

Alex's silence was all the answer she needed.

Shantara paced around the cramped room. "Alex, I knew it was a mistake taking a loan from him, but I didn't know where else to turn. The bank had already turned me down, and I was in real danger of losing the store."

"What made you go to him?"

"I knew he had money to burn, Alex. Jefferson had more things going on that just his blacksmithing."

Alex said gently, "So you let him get a foothold in your store."

Shantara wrung her hands together. "Alex, you'd better believe I regretted every second of it! There were no papers drawn up, nothing legal, anyway, just an IOU from me to him. It made my skin crawl, the way he'd come into my store and act like it was his. Alex, that's the main reason I created this fair! It was the only way I could get him off my back. I had some of the money, and the proceeds from the fair would have covered the rest."

Alex studied her carefully. "There's more to this that you're not telling me."

Shantara moved to the window, refusing to meet his gaze. She didn't confirm or deny Alex's accusation immediately.

After a few moments, she said, "Alex, I'm honestly scared."

"Go on," Alex said softly.

In a shaking voice, Shantara said, "When I told Jefferson I was finally going to be able to pay him off, he said I wasn't taking the extra interest into consideration. He was trying to extort more money from me, Alex. He was threatening to take my shop."

"So what did you say?"

Shantara sighed deeply, then admitted, "I told him if he tried to collect, I'd kill him."

Alex couldn't believe what he was hearing. "Was anyone else around when you said it, Shantara?"

She nodded glumly. "It happened in my store, Alex. A dozen people probably heard me. I didn't exactly lower my voice when I threatened him. I was upset."

Alex had to admit that his friend certainly had gotten herself into a jam.

After a few moments of thought, Alex said, "Here's

what I'd do if I were you. Keep this loan arrangement to yourself. It's not going to do you any good volunteering the information to the sheriff. He's got a one-track mind, and you don't want it focused on you."

"What if he asks me about it later? Won't it look like I'm trying to hide something if I don't come clean now?"

Alex walked to her side. "Shantara, if you tell him now, he's bound to get suspicious. Let me dig into this some more. Your arrangement may never come to light."

Shantara leaned over and kissed him quickly on the cheek.

"What was that for?" Alex asked.

"For not asking me if I killed him. Thanks for believing in me, Alex."

"You're welcome. Now let me see what I can find out."

There was a knock on the door. Alex opened it, and Sandra Beckett walked into the small space.

"I'm not interrupting anything, am I?" Sandra asked.

Shantara said, "No, I was just leaving. I've got to get back to the fair." Without another word, Shantara left the room.

"What was that all about?" Sandra asked.

"We were just covering a few things about the fair," he lied. Changing the subject, Alex asked, "Did you have any luck with the sheriff?"

Sandra nodded. "That's what I came by to tell you. Armstrong's released Bill Yadkin, at least for the moment. He warned Bill not to leave town, but the sheriff knows he's going to have to come up with more evidence before he can charge him with murder. Our sheriff told me to let you know he'll be here shortly to finish interviewing suspects. I've got a feeling he'll be trying to find some corroborating evidence to nail our young blacksmith friend."

Sandra paused at the door as she was leaving, trailing one hand on the frame. "Alex, if you need to talk, just give me a call. I know it could get lonely without Elise here."

"Everything's fine," he said impatiently.

She said, "I'm not doubting it for an instant. Just remember, sometimes it helps to have a friend nearby."

Before he could reply, she was gone. How had Sandra already picked up on the fact that Elise was gone? That's when he remembered that Betsy Jenkins, the town's only travel agent, was Sandra's secretary's sister-in-law. There was no doubt in Alex's mind that as soon as the ticket had been ordered, a follow-up telephone call went out. That was just great. Soon everyone in town would think she'd abandoned him.

Elise's absence was going to be a hardship, there was no doubt about that. Alex wasn't sure how in the world he was going to run Hatteras West single-handedly and solve Jefferson Lee's murder at the same time, but he was going to give it everything he had.

He had given Shantara his word.

8

By the time Sheriff Armstrong showed up, Alex was nearly finished folding another load of towels fresh from the dryer. Elise had taken care of cleaning the rooms before she'd gone, but he still had a great deal to do if he was going to keep his guests happy.

"You have a second?" the sheriff asked. His tone was the nicest it had been in days.

Alex finished folding the last towel. "Absolutely. I heard you released Bill Yadkin."

Armstrong said, "Let's just say I'm looking at all my options before I jump one way or another. I don't want to do anything official until I'm ready."

"What can I do for you, Sheriff?"

"Do you mind if I use your office again? I want to talk to that pottery couple, the woodworking lady and the weaver, too. I never had a chance to get to them earlier."

Alex nodded. "Sure, you know you're welcome to it. Is there any chance I can sit in on the interviews?" he asked casually.

"Normally I'd be okay with that, Alex, but I'd rather do this in private, if you don't mind."

"I understand," Alex said, trying to hide his disappointment. He would rather have been included in the interviews, but he'd been present before only by Sheriff Armstrong's grace, and it looked like he'd used up his share of it, at least for the moment.

"Don't worry, I'll track you down before I go and let you know what happened," Armstrong said as he walked out the door.

Alex made sure he had plenty to do in the main lobby the rest of the day. He wasn't spying; there truly was dusting and sweeping to do, but he did want to be close when the suspects left. If he was really lucky, he might even overhear something. At this point, anything would help.

Evans was in his chair as Alex worked, watching the world pass him by outside the inn's windows.

"Young man, I envy you," Evans said as Alex dusted off a collection of lanterns his grandfather had amassed. They were displayed prominently in one corner of the lobby on a stand Alex's father had built just for them.

"Grab a rag, Evans, there's plenty of dusting for everyone," Alex said, smiling.

The older man chuckled. "I don't mean I envy your daily tasks, I'm referring more to this life you lead. Interesting people traipse in and out of your life on a daily basis, and you have a beautiful home to live in with a wondrous lighthouse next door. You've truly got it all, young man."

Alex refrained from adding the realities of being an innkeeper: blocked toilets at two in the morning, guests who believed if it wasn't nailed down it was free for the taking, and all of the bone-wearying, mind-numbing work that had to be started fresh each and every day. In spite of it, not because of it, Alex loved Hatteras West, but he was also very aware of the tremendous amount of work involved in keeping it afloat. The fact that Evans Graile, a guest, sat enjoying the beautiful day while Alex, the innkeeper, worked steadily away punctuated the point more than anything he could ever say.

"It's a good life, Evans," he agreed, meaning it deep in his heart.

Alex heard raised voices coming from his office, so he moved to the front desk a few paces away from his door, where he pretended to go over the register receipts as he listened in.

The voices were suddenly much clearer now. Jenny Harris was in the office with Sheriff Armstrong, and from the sound of it, there was quite a battle going on.

Alex saw the knob on his door spin. It gave him just enough time to bury his nose in the register before the door opened.

"You know where to find me," Jenny snapped at the sheriff as she stormed past Alex without even a nod.

Armstrong walked over to Alex, shaking his head. "She always was a little high-strung, wasn't she?"

Alex knew that better than Armstrong ever would. "I take it she objected to your line of questioning," he said with a slight grin.

It defused the tension in Armstrong's face. "You might say that. She's got to realize I know she was dating Jefferson Lee as recently as a few months ago. Of *course* she's going to be a suspect on my list."

Alex had known about Jenny and Jefferson; the two had struck him as an odd pairing, but love was sometimes indiscriminate in the couples it brought together.

Armstrong said, "Alex, I wouldn't say no to a soda. You have any in your fridge?"

Alex nodded. "Help yourself. In fact, I think I'll join you." He retrieved two drinks, thought about offering Evans one, but realized the man would never consume anything but his special blend of tea.

Besides, Alex wanted some time alone to pump the sheriff.

As they drank their sodas in his office, Alex asked, "So how do things look?"

"There are just too many people who had a reason to hate that man! I never cared for Lee myself, but I look like one of his biggest fans compared to what I've heard these last few days. I don't care if he was a real slug; he didn't deserve to die the way he did."

"Nobody does," Alex agreed. "So, the husband-and-wife potters are next, right?"

Armstrong nodded. "I think I want to tackle them one at a time. Would you do me a favor, Alex? Would you go get one of them, I don't care which one, and tell them I want to see them? I need to make a phone call while you're doing that."

"Sure thing," Alex said. It would give him a chance to talk with the potters, and perhaps that would even help in his own investigation.

Marilynn Baxter was working on the potter's wheel, forming the clay gracefully into a bowl right before Alex's eyes. The spinning motion of the shifting clay was mesmerizing. How did she do it? He watched another minute before approaching Craig Monroe.

Instead of the summons he'd been ordered to give, Alex said, "She's really good, isn't she?"

Craig nodded absently. "One of the best I've ever seen, including me. I just wish . . ."

"What," Alex prodded.

"Nothing," Craig said abruptly as he moved back to a drying rack starting to fill up with gray-shaded pieces. There were all kinds of items displayed there, from pitchers to bowls to plates to whimsical little pinched figures, all made of clay.

Craig was just moving a bowl when Alex said, "By the way, the sheriff sent me out to get you."

"That's right," Craig said as he nearly dropped the bowl. "He said he wanted to talk to us."

"One at a time," Alex added.

That brought a burnish to Craig's cheeks. "We talk to him together, or we don't talk to him at all!"

Alex said, "Hey, don't take it out on me, I'm just the messenger."

Craig walked over to Marilynn and said something Alex couldn't hear. Her hands faltered for a moment, and the delicate structure collapsed.

She tried to make a joke of it as the onlookers gasped. "Earth to earth, and all that," she said as she peeled the remnants of the clay off the wheel. "That's all for now, folks. We're going to take a little break. Don't forget, everything you see behind me is for sale."

As Marilynn cleaned her hands in a bucket of water, she said, "I'll get Shantara to watch the booth while we're gone. We can't make any money if we don't have anybody here selling our wares."

Craig said, "The sheriff wants us one at a time, and he wants to see us now!"

"He's just going to have to wait," Marilynn said calmly. "Shantara! Could you come over here?"

Shantara joined them and readily agreed to take over their sales while they were gone.

As the three of them walked to the inn, Alex said, "I don't know what the sheriff's going to say about this. He only asked me to get one of you."

Craig started to snap a retort when Marilynn put a hand on his shoulder, "He's in luck. Today's special is two potters for the price of one."

Alex said, "Do you mind me asking how well you two knew Jefferson Lee?"

Did Craig flinch at the question? He couldn't tell for sure; the hot afternoon sun was in his eyes.

Marilynn stepped in and said, "We've done a few fairs with him in North Carolina and parts of Tennessee, but we traveled a lot more than he did."

Craig grunted, "Jefferson liked to stay close to home. For everything."

The man was definitely on edge. Alex decided it might be a good time to give him a shove. "Did you have any reason to hate him, Craig?"

The man started to speak when Marilynn interrupted coolly, "Who's running this investigation, Alex, you or the sheriff?"

"The sheriff is, of course. I just couldn't help wondering about it from the way your husband's been acting."

"It's none of your business then, is it," Craig said before Marilynn could stop him.

"You're absolutely right," Alex agreed, smiling.

They were on the front porch by then, and the couple hurried in ahead of him.

Armstrong didn't look all that surprised that they'd come together.

"I just need one of you right now. That way the other can go back to your booth," he said.

Marilynn said, "That won't be a problem. We have someone watching it for us. Don't you think it would be more efficient if you talked with both of us at the same time?"

"Ma'am, I'll do it my way, if you please. Since you're so eager to talk, why don't you go on in first?"

Craig started to say something, but Marilynn cut him off yet again. It was a wonder the man ever got to say anything. "Let's get this over with, Sheriff, I have a living to earn." Marilynn turned to Craig. "Why don't you go back to the booth? I'll come get you when the sheriff's ready for you."

Craig obviously wasn't thrilled with the plan, but Alex could see there was no room for debate. The potter stormed past Alex and slammed the door on his way out.

Marilynn said, "You'll have to forgive him. Craig hasn't been sleeping well lately."

"He can join the club," the sheriff said. "Murder gives me insomnia, too."

As they disappeared into his office, Alex couldn't help feeling that Armstrong was wasting his breath with Marilynn Baxter. She was too cool to let anything slip. He would love to hear the sheriff's interview with Craig Monroe, though. That should prove to be very interesting.

As predicted, Marilynn's time with the sheriff was brief, and from the look on Armstrong's face, not all that productive.

After she left in search of her husband, Armstrong said, "That woman missed her calling. She should have been a lawyer." There was no admiration in his voice as he said it.

"Maybe you'll have more luck with her husband."

"I doubt it. By the time she's through with him, I doubt I'll be able to get him to admit his own name."

As predicted, by the time the sheriff got Craig in Alex's office, the man was as silent as the nearby mountains. Armstrong shook his head sadly as Craig left the lobby.

"Well, that was purely a waste of breath."

Alex asked, "What now?"

"It's time I talked with our lady woodworker. I've been putting it off, since Rachel blew up at me, but I've got to interview her. She's strong as an ox, and I don't relish making her any madder at me than she already is."

Alex smiled. "Just another benefit of being sheriff."

"I'd send you to get her if I thought she'd come, but I've got a feeling she isn't exactly eager to talk to me."

A few minutes later, Rachel came back in with the sheriff. He'd been wrong about one thing; she was perfectly willing to talk to him. In fact, from the sound of it, Armstrong wasn't going to be able to get a question in between the verbal attacks. Alex was truly glad he wasn't in the sheriff's shoes.

Alex touched the woodworker's shoulder lightly to say something when she grabbed his hand and pulled it off her. She was strong! When she saw that it was Alex, she immediately released her grip. "Sorry, I didn't know it was you."

Alex fought the urge to rub the feeling back into his hand as he said, "Take it easy, Rachel. Sheriff Armstrong wants the same thing as you do, to find out who killed Jefferson Lee."

"Well it certainly wasn't Bill," she snapped.

"So answer his questions and help him move on."

Rachel took a breath, then said, "Of course you're right, Alex. I'm sorry I snapped at you."

She turned to the sheriff and said, "Let's get this over with. Aren't you coming?"

As she stepped into Alex's office, Armstrong said, "Thanks."

"My pleasure."

After the door closed, Alex briskly rubbed the stiffness out of his hand. He'd had no idea looking at Rachel just how strong she was. An unwelcome thought crept into his mind. She would have had plenty of strength to drive that spear into Jefferson Lee's chest. He had discounted the women up front, not thinking they had the physical power to accomplish it, but it was time to reconsider. Added to that was the fact that Jefferson Lee had been her boyfriend's rival, intent on destroying the young blacksmith's career. Had Rachel decided to take matters into her own hands? It was a possibility well worth considering.

She was much meeker when she left Alex's office, even offering him a nod and a slight smile as she walked past.

Alex found Armstrong at his desk. "Have any luck?"

The sheriff threw his hands up. "Nobody's seen anything or done anything around here at all. They're nothing but a bunch of innocent lambs."

"So where does that leave you?"

Armstrong leaned back in Alex's chair, and the seat protested. The sheriff said, "I've interviewed all my suspects out here. It's time to catch up with Irene and see if she's come up with anything." As Alex walked him to the squad car, the sheriff said, "I'll be in touch, Alex." Getting into his car, he said awkwardly, "By the way, I was sorry to hear about Elise."

"She's not gone forever, Sheriff. She was called away on a family emergency."

"Uh-huh," the sheriff said quickly as he started the engine.

After he was gone, Alex watched the trail of dust from the squad car as it sped down the lane. Why was everyone so quick to assume that Elise was gone for good?

Were they jumping to conclusions, or did all of Elkton Falls know something that he didn't?

He went back into his office and saw something sparkling in one corner near the copier. Alex retrieved a bracelet, swung it on two fingers, then put it in his pocket. It looked familiar, and he was sure Elise must have dropped it when she'd been cleaning his office. It only made him realize more how much he missed her.

But he couldn't dwell on her departure. He had an inn to run, and as if that wasn't enough, he'd promised Shantara he'd find the murderer.

There just weren't enough hours in a day.

9

Alex was relieved when the fair was finally over for the evening, the crowds of visitors gone at last. One more day and it would be finished. A part of him regretted agreeing to let Shantara hold the fair at the inn, particularly during the Lighthouse Lighting festivities, but he knew in his heart that he'd honestly had no other choice. The lighting was scheduled for tomorrow night's closing ceremonies, but for the first time since he'd taken over The Hatteras West Inn, he wasn't eager to fire up the Fresnel lens. The murder had thrown a dark cloud over everything, and Alex wasn't looking forward to hitting the switch at all.

It didn't help that Elise would miss it, too.

It was stressful enough running Hatteras West by himself without the added traffic of visitors wandering through the inn during the day. He'd caught one woman actually trying to sneak out the front door with one of the lanterns displayed in the lobby just as the fair was shutting down for the day. She dropped the lantern when he'd caught her, shattering the glass in it. Alex had been so shocked by her actions that he'd just stood there as she raced out the door without her prize.

It was the last straw. Alex cleaned up the mess, carefully searching the floor to make sure he hadn't missed any errant pieces of glass. After he was certain he'd retrieved every last sliver, Alex posted a hastily scrawled sign on the front door that said Guests Only in bold, thick letters.

Evans Graile, back from one of his rare forays into the world, shook his head when he saw the sign. "Not very welcoming, is it, Alex?"

"Sorry, but this fair is driving me crazy."

Evans smiled gently. "Ah, but look what a spectacle it's provided for me. I can't remember the last time I saw so many people without ever having to leave my chair."

"I'm glad you're happy," Alex said as he adjusted the sign. He probably should have used something stronger to tack it in place; someone would probably walk off with his sign as a souvenir.

Evans went on, "To be honest with you, it's a real shame it's all ending tomorrow night, Alex. I don't know what I'll do for entertainment after everyone else is gone."

Alex said, "We've got checkers, chess, books, hiking trails, Bear Rocks, and don't forget the lighthouse itself."

Graile shook his head sadly. "I'm afraid most of those things are a little too strenuous for me, Alex. Besides, I like to watch. I'm not a big fan of actually participating."

Alex was saved from responding as Jenny hurried up to him. "Can we talk?"

"Sure," Alex said as he led her inside. Evans Graile

was close on his tracks. That man wasn't about to miss a thing!

Much to the older man's disappointment, Alex said, "Why don't we talk in my office? I'm still going through a pile of mail I haven't gotten around to yet."

"Anywhere is fine with me," she agreed as they walked inside. Jenny made a point of closing the door behind her, and Alex was surprised when she slid the barrel lock in place as well.

"What can I do for you?" he asked.

"You can start by forgiving me," Jenny said as she stepped closer. "I know what you must think of me after the foolish way I acted earlier."

Alex took a step back. "There's nothing to forgive. This murder has everybody out of sorts."

She said gently, "I still don't know what got into me." Jenny smiled slightly. "Alex, should I be offended you weren't even tempted by my offer of reconciliation?"

"No ma'am, that's not it at all. Honestly, it's got nothing to do with you," Alex said.

"You're telling me that there's not even the slightest chance of us going out again?"

He hadn't meant to hurt her feelings, but he obviously had. Alex said softly, "On a date? No, but I'd be happy to do something with you as a friend. I'm sorry."

Jenny said lightly, "Oh well. I suppose Elise must have something to do with it. She really is quite lovely, isn't she?"

"Jenny, there's nothing going on between us. Our relationship is strictly business. Elise is on leave handling a family medical emergency. As soon as it resolves itself, she'll be back at Hatteras West. Why is everyone—" His words were cut off by the telephone.

"Excuse me," Alex said as he answered, "The Hatteras West Inn."

"Hi Alex, it's Elise. I just got in."

"It's good to hear your voice. Can you hold on one second?" He covered the mouthpiece and told Jenny, "I'm sorry, but I need to take this."

Jenny nodded as she quietly left the room, closing the door behind her. As soon as she was gone, Alex bolted it. He wasn't in the mood for any interruptions. "Sorry about that. So how's your dad doing?"

"He's scared, Alex. It just about breaks my heart to see a man as strong as he is so afraid."

"How's your mom holding up?"

Elise laughed softly. "She's already tried to feed me twice since I walked in the door. I swear, if I hang around here too long, I'm not going to be able to fit into any of my clothes. Any new developments on the murder?"

"Nothing I've been able to pick up on. Armstrong's playing this one pretty close to the vest. Listen, you shouldn't be worrying about that, Elise. You've got enough on your mind."

"Believe me, I could use the distraction. This place is like a big empty cave without any guests."

Alex knew Elise's parents ran an inn much like his own, with one important exception: there was no lighthouse on their property. "What happened to everybody?"

"Mom canceled all our reservations until we get through this. There were only a few people scheduled, and they've all been staying here for years, so they understood. Alex, I know I need to be here, but I still feel guilty about leaving you like I did."

Alex started to say something when he heard a

strong male voice in the background calling to her, "Elise, we need to go now!"

"Emergency?" Alex asked, concerned.

"Nothing like that, but I'd better say good-bye. I'll talk to you later."

"Keep me posted," Alex said to dead air.

The conversation with Elise had done nothing to ease his mind. It seemed like she'd barely thought of him since she'd left. That male voice in the background had to be her fiancé, Peter Asheford.

Alex knew he had to stop feeling sorry for himself as he hung up the phone. Her father was going into major surgery. Of course she needed to be there with him. As for Peter Asheford, he had every right to be there as well. No matter how much he wished otherwise, Elise was engaged to another man. But he knew in his heart that she was coming back; Hatteras West had a hold on her.

What Alex had to do was to stop listening to all the tongue wagging in Elkton Falls and get on with his life.

After a sandwich and a glass of ice-cold milk, Alex decided to walk the grounds to see how badly they'd been trampled by all of the visitors to the fair. The heavy turnout was a real boon for Shantara, but it had been nothing short of a nightmare for him. Alex was beginning to envy Lucius Crane's wisdom in refusing to hold the fair on his farm.

The first thing that struck Alex as he walked the grounds was the unbelievable amount of litter. His once-pristine land was covered with the debris from the day: discarded wrappers, packages, soda cans, and the other flotsam and jetsam from the wave of people who had passed through.

As he started to pick up the first piece of trash, he heard a car horn behind him. Shantara was leading a cavalcade of the worst collection of cars, trucks and vans he'd ever seen in his life.

As she popped out of her station wagon, Shantara said, "Alex, that's not your job. I've got my crew here. Sorry we're late."

"I just couldn't stand seeing my land like this."

As the young people filed out of their vehicles, Shantara said, "Don't worry, Alex, we'll have this mess cleaned up in no time. You're in for a treat. These kids are good." She turned to the gathered young men and women. "Okay, let's jump on this. Get your trash bags from Emily, and drop them off at Byron's truck when they're full." As the crew started toward the mess buzzing and laughing, Shantara called out to them, "Remember, recycle everything you can."

They fell on the fairground in a crashing wave, laughing and working as they moved through the grass like a horde of human vacuum cleaners.

"What are you paying your crew?" he asked.

"Minimum wage and pizza at Mama Ravolini's as a bonus. They were happy to get the work."

Alex said, "From the look of this crowd, I'd say they're going to break you with the pizza offer."

Shantara smiled. "Irma Bean's giving me the pizzas at cost, and the kids only get the bonus if they work both days. I'll do all right." It was amazing how quickly the teens cleaned up after the fairgoers, though the trampled grass wouldn't be as easy to restore.

"Alex, don't worry about the grass. I've got enough left in the budget to reseed this area," Shantara said, reading his mind.

"I've got it covered. I'd been planning to do it myself anyway. So, are you happy with the results of all
your hard work?"

"I guess so. Alex, one of the best reasons I came up
with this idea was to expose people to the old ways of
doing things. It wasn't *just* a way to make money.
There are skills that are being lost every day, and we're
not doing nearly enough to preserve them."

Alex said, "Easy, girl, it was just a question. You
don't have to convert me."

Shantara frowned. "It's just so frustrating. I imagined people coming out here to see the demonstrations,
to even try their hands at a few of the crafts them-
selves, and instead they've flocked here to see the murder scene! You want to hear something ghoulish?
Jefferson Lee's stuff sold like crazy as soon as everyone found out about the murder. He had a college girl
working his booth, and she kept right on selling everything, even after he was dead!"

"Did Jefferson have any family left? I didn't know
him all that well."

"There's a sister in Hickory; she'll be coming tomorrow. Callie told me she wasn't all that surprised
when she found out her brother had been killed."

Alex said, "From what I've been hearing lately, I
can't say I'm all that surprised, either." Alex shook
himself. "Don't mind me, I'm out of sorts tonight for
some reason."

"It's got to be hard on you, with Elise gone."

Alex exploded. "Why does everyone think she's
gone for good? She's visiting her parents on a medical
emergency! Shantara, I swear to you, she's coming
back to Hatteras West!"

She looked startled by his outburst. "Easy, Alex, I

just meant it had to be tough on you running the inn by yourself until she gets back."

He laughed softly. "Sorry, it's just that everyone I've talked to today has made it sound like she's gone forever. You wouldn't believe Jenny Harris. She wants us to start dating again."

Shantara said disdainfully, "It doesn't surprise me in the least. I know you two used to go out, Alex, but you're better off without her."

"It sounds like you're a little jealous yourself," he said, smiling.

She laughed just a little too loud and too long for Alex's ego to take.

He said gruffly, "Okay, you made your point."

"Nothing personal, Alex, but you're not my type."

"And just what is your type?"

She pretended to think about it a minute, then said, "Let's see, he's got to be strong, handsome, rich, don't forget a good sense of humor—"

Alex cut her off. "You're not asking for much, are you? And you think you're going to meet this Prince Charming in Elkton Falls?"

"Where there's breath, there's hope," Shantara said with a twinkle in her eye.

A young girl with a long ponytail poking out the back of her baseball cap said, "We're done here, Shantara. The gang wanted me to ask you if there was any chance we could get an early start on that pizza party."

"Sorry, Emily, you know the deal; no pizza until the end of the fair, and that's not until tomorrow night."

Emily winked at her and whispered, "I told them that's what you'd say, but the boys insisted I ask anyway."

"I understand completely."

After the kids poured back into their cars, Alex had

to admit the place did look a thousand percent better than it had before they'd arrived.

He only wished the fair was over now, instead of having to go through it all again tomorrow.

Alex patted Shantara's shoulder gently and asked, "Would you like to come in? I've got a bottle of wine and two comfortable chairs just calling our names."

"Don't tempt me. If I did that, I'd never make it home."

"We had a cancellation, so I've got a spare room, if you're interested. You're welcome to stay at the inn tonight."

"No offense, Alex, but I need to get away from Hatteras West for a little while."

"Not a problem," he said.

Alex was walking Shantara to her car when there was a frantic wail from the front porch as the door slammed.

"My wife is gone! Somebody's kidnapped her!" Craig Monroe stood there, outlined in the moonlight, a look of complete and utter despair on his face.

It appeared that the evil visiting Hatteras West was still somewhere lurking on the grounds.

10

Alex ran up onto the porch, with Shantara not far behind. "How do you know she's been kidnapped, Craig? Did you find a note?"

"No," Craig snapped, "but she told me to meet her in our room an hour ago, and she's not there."

Shantara said calmly, "Craig, she probably just got held up talking to someone on the grounds. I'm sure she's around here somewhere."

"You don't understand. Her insulin is still in the minifridge. She's got to have it, and it's something Marilynn's not about to forget or put off. I'm telling you, the only way she'd miss an injection is if somebody kidnapped her. Call the sheriff, Alex! He needs to get right on this!"

Alex said, "Craig, I know you're worried, but Armstrong's not going to do anything based on what you can tell him right now. He's going to want something a little more concrete. You need to call home and see if your wife's there. Then check around and see if there's anywhere else she could be: with friends, family, anybody you can think of. In the meantime, I'll take a look around the property and see if I can find her."

Shantara chimed in, "I'll help you, Alex."

Craig nodded abruptly as he rushed back into the inn. "Hurry. We've got to find her. She has to have that insulin."

Alex headed for the lighthouse as Shantara said, "Do you think she's really up *there*?"

Alex shook his head. "I doubt it, but it's still the best observation point around. If she's anywhere nearby, we should have a good chance of spotting her."

Alex's gaze went to the new construction as he hurried past. He would have to search there more thoroughly if Marilynn didn't turn up soon, but it was something he'd rather put off. One body found on the site in the last twenty-four hours was more than enough for him. There was a reason besides kidnapping that could keep Marilynn from her insulin.

That was if she was past needing it.

Alex and Shantara climbed the lighthouse steps at a fierce pace, leaving little breath for conversation. As Alex opened the door at the top, they stepped out onto the observation platform and started walking slowly around, intent on finding any sign of Marilynn. The breeze had picked up and was pressing against him like a ghostly hand. Alex usually loved heavy winds at Hatteras West, but as the sky began to darken, all he cared about was finding the potter. The inn looked like a dollhouse from so high above, and the new construction looked like a precocious child had started a building with sticks but had grown bored with the process and had given up. Alex could see parts of Bear Rocks from the railing, but much of the rock formation was hidden by a thick band of trees that separated it from the main buildings.

There was no sign of Marilynn anywhere.

They made the circuit twice around the observation platform when they met again near the door.

"Anything?" Shantara asked.

"Not a thing," Alex admitted. "I couldn't see most of Bear Rocks, though. There's a chance she could be there."

"Let's go look, then."

As they hurried down the stairs to the top landing, Alex paused at the window and said, "I want to see if there's anything we missed."

They both peered out each of the narrow windows, but they couldn't see anything that would help.

On the way down, Shantara asked, "Alex, do you honestly think Marilynn Baxter's been kidnapped? What possible reason could anyone have for grabbing her?"

"I don't have the slightest clue. To be honest with you, I believe Craig's overreacting, but I could be wrong. I couldn't even guess why anyone would kidnap his wife. They don't have a lot of money, do they?"

"No, they both work real jobs to support their pottery studio. I can't imagine them having anything anybody else would want."

As Alex started down the steps again, he said, "Well, Craig must think so, or he wouldn't have immediately assumed she'd been kidnapped. Unless . . ."

"Unless what?" Shantara asked, breathing hard from the climb down.

"Unless he's afraid the reality of what might have happened to her is worse," Alex said, voicing his earlier fear.

Shantara paused a few steps until she asked her next

question. "You don't honestly think something's happened to her, do you, Alex?"

"I wish I knew, but I can't deny it's a possibility. I've got a feeling in the pit of my stomach that something's wrong."

As they finally reached the bottom, Shantara said, "No offense, but I hope you're mistaken."

"Believe me, so do I."

Craig met them as they approached the inn. "Did you find her?" he asked breathlessly.

"Not yet. I take it she wasn't at any of the places you called," Alex said.

"We don't have that many friends," Craig said brusquely. "Nobody's seen her."

Alex looked over at the new construction. "There's a chance she could be there."

Craig yelled, "Marilynn! Marilynn!"

There was no response.

Craig waited a few moments, then said, "Obviously she's not there, or she would have answered me."

Alex said, "Craig, why don't you go work the phones some more. Shantara and I have a few more places to check."

"Forget that. I'm coming with you."

Alex stopped him dead in his tracks. "Listen, we might find something you're not going to want to see."

The man flushed for a second, then said, "I need to know, Alex. She's my wife."

As they walked through the growing twilight toward the new construction, Alex kept a constant vigil for anything out of the ordinary.

With real sighs of relief, they found that the construction site was empty. Alex had silently dreaded finding another exhibitor pinned against a post. Could it be that Jefferson Lee's murder was connected to the disappearance of Marilynn Baxter? Or was Marilynn gone for another, entirely different reason? There were too many unanswered questions buzzing around Alex's head.

"What's next?" Craig asked.

"Bear Rocks is the only other place on the property she could be."

"She wouldn't just stay out there, Alex, not in the dark."

"Wait right here," Alex said as he went into the inn. Evans Graile was still sitting in his chair, a bright glow lighting his face. "Isn't this awful? A kidnapping! Imagine that!"

"Evans, we're not sure what's happened yet. Would you like to join the search party?" Alex asked as he retrieved two flashlights from the front desk. He kept them stashed there for guests when thunderstorms knocked out the inn's power, something that happened more frequently than he cared to admit.

"I'd better stay here in case there's a call from the kidnappers," he said a little too brightly for Alex's taste.

"You do that," Alex said brusquely as he moved for the door.

He could tell Evans was unhappy about the tone Alex had used with him. One of Alex's most important rules as an innkeeper was to hold his tongue and his attitude when it came to his guests, but he was truly beginning to be concerned about Marilynn Baxter's well-being.

Before Alex could leave, Evans said contritely, "You know I don't want anything to happen to that poor girl. It's just that normally I don't get much excitement in my life."

Alex nodded and tried to force a smile. "Then stick around; something's always going on at Hatteras West."

He offered one of the flashlights to Craig and Shantara. "Sorry, I just have one spare, and nobody knows Bear Rocks like I do."

Shantara said, "You take it, Craig. I'm going to drive into town and see if anyone's spotted her. Where does she like to go?"

"You could try the studio and the house. The library's closed, or I'd say to go there. The only other place I can think of would be your store."

Shantara nodded. "I'll call Marcie on the way in on my cell phone and find out if she's seen her." Marcie was Shantara's assistant manager, a fancy title since there were just two of them working the general store. It was a lot for two people to handle, since they covered everything from the small post office in one corner to the heavy feeds out back to the pots, pans and assortment of ten thousand other items Shantara had for sale there. Alex thought Marcie would probably be even happier than he would be when the fair was over; she'd been running the store single-handedly for the last week while Shantara prepared for the fair.

"Keep us posted," Alex called out. "Evans is manning the telephone, so he'll let us know if you find her."

"You do the same for me, Alex." She turned to Craig. "Don't worry, she'll turn up soon, I just know it."

Craig grabbed the flashlight from Alex's hand. "I hope you're right."

Some people described Bear Rocks as eerie in the daylight, with the twisting formation of rocks weathered by ages of nature's forces. There were slides, holes and pathways within the stones that formed a magical world Alex had lived in as a child. He still knew every twist and turn of the rocks, every secret passage that led to an unexpected place in the stone forest.

"We'll never find her in there," Craig said.

"Take your flashlight and walk around the edges of the rocks. You can see a lot from where you'll be, so don't give up. I'm going into the heart of the rocks to look there."

"I'm coming with you," Craig said bluntly.

"Listen, if Marilynn's in there, I have a much better chance of finding her alone. I need you to look around the perimeter. I don't have time to argue; just do it."

It was obvious Craig wasn't used to the tone Alex used with him, but Alex had needed to get his attention. Alex turned on his flashlight and slipped through the first path, a slide that led to a side shoot within the formation. Though he was quite a bit older than he'd been when he'd first learned the rocks, his body took over, twisting and crawling in places as he glided over, under and between the stones.

It was more of a workout than he'd ever remembered, and he knew he'd be stiff and sore in the morning, but Alex made record time going over every inch of the interior rocks.

There was nothing there, not a single hint that Marilynn had ever been on Bear Rocks.

One look at Craig's face told him that he hadn't found anything else, either.

Alex had to wonder if Marilynn Baxter truly had been kidnapped after all. If she'd disappeared on her own, where had she gone? And more importantly, why?

11

"So what do we do now?" Craig asked Alex as they hurried back to the inn.

"I'm not sure," Alex answered.

Craig snapped, "I'm not waiting another second. I'm calling Sheriff Armstrong. He's going to come out here whether he likes it or not."

Craig brushed past Alex and nearly slammed the door in his face. Alex walked in and sat down beside Evans Graile in one of the chairs that faced the windows. "I don't suppose you've heard anything, have you?"

"There was only one call. Elise phoned two minutes ago. She said she'd talk to you tomorrow."

Blast it all! Alex wanted to talk to her more than just about anything, and he'd missed her while he was out on a wild-goose chase. "Did she leave a number at the hospital?"

"No, I'm sorry, Alex, she didn't. You could probably track her down, but to be honest with you, she sounded exhausted from her ordeal."

Evans was right; it wouldn't be that hard to find the hospital's number, but Elise hadn't left it, so she most likely was too tired to talk to him. He had to respect her wishes. Since she'd been gone, Alex had found himself unusually moody. He had to keep reminding himself that was sheer nonsense. He'd managed fine before she'd come along, and he'd be all right long after she was gone.

Then why did he feel so empty inside?

Ten minutes later, the sheriff drove up Point Road. Alex knew the man's general disposition before he even got out of the car. If Armstrong believed there was the slightest chance Marilynn Baxter had truly been kidnapped, he would have ripped up the road with lights flashing and siren blaring. As it was, the steady pace of the darkened and silent patrol car told him that Armstrong was there just to appease a constituent.

Alex met him at the patrol car before the sheriff could open his door. Armstrong finished saying something on his radio, then got out and stood beside Alex, leaning against the driver's door.

"I'm surprised Monroe wasn't out here to greet me in person, he was so fired up on the phone," Armstrong said. "Alex, just between you and me, do you honestly think that man believes his wife was kidnapped?"

"He seemed pretty earnest," Alex admitted, "and she is gone, there's no doubt about that. We searched all around the property without any luck."

"From what I've heard around town, this isn't the first time she's wandered off. Far be it for me to spread idle gossip, but—"

Before the sheriff could share the rumor, Craig Monroe burst out through the front door. "It's about time you got here! Where's Irene? Doesn't she usually investigate these things with you?"

"Take it easy, Craig. There's no crime scene, so I didn't see any reason to drag her out here this late. She's not feeling so chipper right now; her arthritis is acting up. We must be in for one whale of a storm in the next few days. Irene's better than the Weather Channel when it comes to predicting storms."

"So who's going to help you investigate?" Craig demanded.

"Hold your horses. We don't even know for sure if a crime's been committed. Did you get a note or a phone call demanding a ransom?"

Craig admitted that he hadn't.

Armstrong went on. "Did anybody see her taken from the property against her will?"

"No, but—"

Armstrong bulled ahead. "So you're going around screaming about a kidnapping without the slightest shred of evidence."

Craig Monroe held up his wife's insulin. "How about this? Why would she leave without her insulin?"

"Is that the only bottle in the world?" the sheriff asked gently.

"Of course it isn't! But I'm telling you, she'd be here if she could!"

The sheriff said calmly, "Tell you what. Why don't we jump in the patrol car and head over to your place. We can check to see if there's any sign of her there. What do you say to that?"

"You're not even going to look around out here first?" Craig snapped.

Armstrong said calmly, "Alex told me you've already searched Hatteras West. Don't you think our time might be better spent looking someplace new?"

Craig reluctantly agreed. "Let me grab my keys. I'll be right back."

As the potter went to retrieve his house keys, the sheriff said, "Now, as I was saying, word around town is that the husband-and-wife team's been having some tough going lately. There's another man, from what I heard at Buck's the other day. First thing I'm going to do is ask around and see if anybody knows who this mystery man is, then I'm going to knock on his door and likely as not, I'll find Ms. Baxter holed up there."

"If that's your plan, do you really want her husband with you?"

Armstrong shrugged. "He raised the alarm, and I doubt I could stop him from coming if I wanted to."

Craig came back out with his keys clutched in his hand. "Let's go."

Alex stepped in. "Are you sure you don't want to stay here? The sheriff will call you the second he finds anything out."

"It's not the same as being there, Alex. I've got to go."

There was no way he was going to change Craig Monroe's mind, so he stepped out of the way and let the man pass.

In a minute, Craig and the sheriff were driving back toward town. Alex saw another car meet them as both vehicles passed going too fast for the narrow lane.

It was Mor and Emma. Good. He could use a couple of friendly faces after all he'd been through that day.

•　　•　　•

"Did you two come all the way out here to baby-sit me?" Alex asked Mor and Emma with a smile after they got out of the car.

"Somebody had to do it," Mor said, returning his grin. "We figured it might as well be us."

"Don't believe a word he says, Alex. We just thought you could use some company," Emma said.

"I appreciate the thought, but I'm a big boy; I'll be fine by myself."

Mor said, "I told you we didn't have to come out here, Emma. If we hurry, we can still make it to Mamma Ravolini's for dinner."

"Mor Pendleton, is that all you ever think about, your stomach?"

Mor hugged her in his bearlike arms. "I can think of a few other things that occupy my thoughts from time to time."

Alex couldn't believe it, but Emma actually blushed. Mor certainly had an effect on her since the two of them hooked up. Alex suddenly felt like the odd man out being in their presence.

Emma said, "Alex, Elise called me this evening and came up with a splendid idea. She suggested I fill in for her here while she's gone. I'd be glad to help out until she gets back."

"Have you given up finding any more emeralds on the land?" Alex asked her.

"No," Emma admitted, "but I could use a break. The geologicals are giving me fits. Working with you at the inn sounds like fun."

Fun? Alex thought of the cleaning, the laundry, the whims of his guests and the thousand other tasks that came with running an inn, but he wasn't about to bring any of them up. Honestly, Alex could use her help.

She'd find out soon enough what she'd gotten herself into. Then he realized he had to be fair with her.

"Are you sure you want to do this?" he asked. "It's a great deal of work."

"It couldn't be much worse than taking care of Mr. Sturbridge, and I did that for more years than I care to remember."

Alex offered his hand. "It's a deal, then. When do you want to start?"

"I'll be here first thing in the morning. How does five A.M. sound?"

"I don't know. I haven't been up that early since I was a kid. I usually don't get started until six-thirty, Emma."

"Tell you what, let's split the difference. I'll be here at six, with bells on." She turned to Mor and said, "We'd better head back into town. I've got a full day ahead of me tomorrow."

Mor winked at Alex, then complained loudly, "I *knew* I'd end up being the one who suffered from this arrangement."

Emma started scolding him. "Mor Pendleton, you can certainly spare a few hours of my company—"

She caught the smile the two men were sharing, then turned her back on them both. "Mor, I'll wait for you in the car. Alex, I'll see you in the morning."

After she was safely ensconced in the car, Alex said, "You two seem to be getting along well."

"Yeah, well, Emma kind of grows on you after a while. She's really something."

"Spare me the details. I'm just glad you're doing all right."

Mor punched Alex gently on the shoulder. In a rare moment of seriousness, he said, "Don't worry about Elise, Alex. I know she's coming back."

"Yeah, I think so, too," Alex said. As he watched Mor drive away, he couldn't help wondering though. It sounded like Elise was settling in for a long stay up north.

Alex hoped Elise planned on coming back, but he had to accept the possibility that she was gone for good. After all, it appeared that she had already lined up a replacement, just in case she decided to stay in West Virginia.

The evening was certainly cool enough, so Alex gladly used it as an excuse to build a fire in the main lobby. He hadn't had enough money to restore the fireplaces in all of the rooms yet, but the massive communal hearth in the lobby had never failed the Winstons in all the generations they'd owned The Hatteras West Inn.

As he reviewed his current situation, he acknowledged that it was a distressing predicament for an innkeeper to be in. One of his guests had been murdered, and another had disappeared without warning. To top it off, the rest of the crafters were leaving tomorrow night after the lighting ceremony, and Alex would be left with a nearly empty inn again. He knew that the first Golden Days Fair would also be the last, certainly as far as Hatteras West was concerned. It was just too much for him, added to his usual hectic life running the inn. When he lit the beacon tomorrow night, it would be a welcome end to something that had started out with so much promise.

As the logs caught fire, Alex decided to use one of the special pieces of firewood one of his guests brought him every year she visited the inn. He loved watching the minerals in the crusted wood ignite in flames of red, gold, green and blue. Alethia Garson brought a stack of driftwood she collected from her home in Buxton on the Outer Banks every time she visited Hatteras West. Alethia was a lighthouse nut; there was no polite way to say it. She'd proudly showed Alex pictures of her own home, filled with every imaginable product ever made in the shape of a lighthouse, from salt and pepper shakers to birdhouses to dinner bells. Without question, though, her proudest possession was a small-scale version of the Cape Hatteras Lighthouse sitting in her own front yard.

Every time he burned a piece of wood from her special stack, Alex thought warmly of her and everyone else who had crossed his threshold to stay at The Hatteras West Inn. Alethia and other guests like her were the real reason Alex continued with the inn when all intelligence told him it was a foolhardy proposition. Not only was Hatteras West the only home he knew, but the people who came back to stay with him year after year were more of a family to him than his own brother had ever been.

As Alex watched the flames, he found himself wondering for the thousandth time who really had murdered Jefferson Lee. Could it actually have been Bill Yadkin, the most obvious suspect, despite Alex's gut feeling? Jalissa Moore, a girl he'd gone to high school with and who now worked as a reporter for Elkton Falls' only newspaper, once told him that one of the first things she'd been taught in journalism school was that if you hear hoofbeats, think horses not zebras.

Bill Yadkin *was* the obvious choice.

But Alex knew that even his good friend Shantara had reasons of her own to want the blacksmith dead.

Did Marilynn Baxter have something to hide concerning the murder? Could she have seen something she shouldn't have? Had she run, or had she been kidnapped, as her husband believed? For that matter, did Craig Monroe know more about her disappearance than he let on?

There was also Jenny to consider. After all, she'd dated the blacksmith recently, and Alex knew firsthand how her moods could swing. How about Rachel? The woodworker was powerful enough, she'd proven it when she'd grabbed his arm, and she was certainly capable of it if she felt her lover was threatened. For that matter, all of the women at the fair were physically strong enough to have done it.

Alex had a thousand questions and not one solid answer for any of them. He wished yet again that Elise was there to talk it all over with him. Even if they didn't come up with a solution on their own, they'd make a go of it, he was certain of that. He pulled the bracelet of hers he'd found from his pocket and toyed with it, wondering what Elise was doing at that very moment.

Chiding himself for his behavior, Alex got up and stoked the fire. As the embers danced upward, Alex tried to clear his mind of murder, kidnapping and Elise.

He didn't have any luck forgetting any of them, not even for a moment.

12

Alex was just about to douse the fire and head off to bed when he heard footsteps coming down the staircase. Who could it be prowling around this late?

Jenny Harris came down the steps dressed in a lacy white nightgown only partially covered by an open silk robe. "I thought I heard someone down here."

Keeping his eyes on the fire, Alex said, "I was just about to call it a night."

She asked softly, "Would you mind keeping me company for a little while?"

Alex didn't feel all that sociable, and he certainly didn't want another discussion with Jenny about their past. He said, "Sorry, but I'm beat."

She stared at him a full ten seconds, and for the life of him, Alex thought she was about to cry.

"What's wrong?" he asked gently.

"I just can't believe how you've been treating me lately," she complained. "Alex, we had something together once, and now it's like you can't even stand being in the same room with me."

"Jenny, it's not that. I like you. I'm just not interested in pursuing it any further than that."

"Okay, I believe you, Alex. Does that mean we can't at least be friends?" Her voice was barely a whisper.

"Friendship is fine with me, as long as that's where it starts and stops," he said.

As Alex started to stand, Jenny leaned forward. "Please, don't go. Alex, I don't want to be alone. Could you stay? Please?"

"Just for a little bit," he agreed reluctantly, "but it really has been a long day."

Staring into the fire, Jenny said, "Alex, these past few days have been like some kind of nightmare. I can't believe Jefferson's dead, can you?"

"I hate the idea of anybody being murdered, especially at Hatteras West, but I didn't know him as well as you did."

Jenny started to cry softly, and Alex couldn't just sit there and coldly watch her tears. He moved beside her and put his arm around her shoulders, offering comfort in the only way he knew how. Jenny instinctively turned to him, burying her head into his chest. There was nothing false or manipulative or even sexual about it. The woman genuinely needed a friend. Ironically, as the sobs finally subsided, Alex was suddenly very much aware of Jenny's physical presence.

As he started for the other couch, she said, "Hold me just a little longer."

"I can't." It was obvious she needed someone to cling to, but it couldn't be him. For the first time since she'd been gone, Alex was just as happy that Elise wasn't there to see this.

Suddenly the front door opened. Jenny still had her

hand on his arm. Alex jumped up and found Rachel Seabock standing at the door, a surprised look on her face.

"Excuse me, I didn't mean to interrupt," she said as she started past them.

"You didn't," Alex said a little too loudly. "We were just enjoying the fire. Why don't you join us?"

Averting her eyes, Rachel said, "Thanks, but I'm going straight to bed. I've been looking all over Elkton Falls for Bill, but I couldn't find him anywhere."

"There's a lot of that going around," Alex said.

"Is Elise missing, too?" Rachel asked.

Obviously she was the only person left in all of Elkton Falls who didn't know Elise had gone to West Virginia. "No," Alex said, "she was called away for a family emergency."

Rachel's eyebrows rose as she asked, "So who else is missing?"

"That's right, you haven't been around. Craig Monroe is under the impression that his wife was kidnapped this evening. The sheriff thinks she's shacking up with her mystery lover. I think they both have overactive imaginations."

Rachel shook her head. "What's happening around here, Alex?"

"It's not Hatteras West's fault," Alex said.

"I'm not blaming you, but this Golden Days Fair has turned out to be a real nightmare." She stared at the fire a second, then said, "I'm going to bed."

"Me, too," Alex said before Rachel could leave. As he moved to kill the fire, Jenny said, "I think I'll stay up a little longer, if you don't mind."

"Good night, then," Alex said while he still had a chaperone. It wasn't that he didn't trust himself to be alone with Jenny; it was just that the woman seemed to know the right strings to pull to get to him. At least this would be her last night at Hatteras West, since the fair was shutting down tomorrow.

Alex dead-bolted his door after he closed it behind him. He suffered through a miserable night of sleep, missing Elise but remembering the smell of Jenny's hair.

Alex woke up grumpy the next morning, having tossed and turned all night, fighting off nightmare steel lances rushing toward him in his sleep. Alex knew he was a real bear without the proper amount of rest, and he always tried to get at least eight hours every night, but as an innkeeper that wasn't always possible, not by a long shot. He wasn't normally a coffee drinker, but this morning he made an exception and brewed up a pot. Elise had been after him to start offering at least bagels, fruit and some juice to their guests each morning, and Alex realized he'd been wrong to stubbornly fight her on it. Starting tomorrow, he'd implement her suggestion. He just hoped she came back to see it.

Alex was just finishing his second cup of coffee when there was a hearty knock on his door.

Emma Sturbridge, dressed in neatly pressed but well-worn jeans and a faded flannel shirt, was ready to start work.

"Morning, Alex. Point me to today's to-do list, and I'll get started."

"Would you like a cup of coffee first?" Alex asked.

"No time for that," Emma said stoutly. "There's work to be done."

Alex laughed and felt his earlier bad mood lifting. Emma was a dose of energy, and that was exactly what he needed at the moment. "We can't get started on the rooms yet, no one's up, but we've got more laundry from yesterday I didn't get around to and all of the floors in the common rooms need sweeping."

"I'm on it," Emma said, bustling off toward the small laundry room in back.

Alex said, "Let me grab a quick bite, then I'll join you."

Emma waved her hand in the air. "Take your time, Alex, I've got the situation well in hand."

There was a crackling competency about Emma Sturbridge, and Alex was suddenly glad Elise had made arrangements for Emma to help out. Certainly he'd rather have Elise working with him, but Emma was the next best thing.

Alex had a quick bowl of cereal and was heading to the laundry room to help Emma, when Jenny came down the stairs dressed in another brightly woven dress she'd made herself. She looked carefully at him as she said, "Alex, I want to thank you for last night. Your company meant the world to me."

"You're welcome, Jenny. I'm always here for my friends."

She took his hand and squeezed it. "We *are* friends, aren't we, Alex? Despite everything that's happened between us in the past and my behavior these last few days."

"Absolutely," Alex said. "Now, if you'll excuse me, I've got a basket full of sheets to fold."

Jenny said softly, "You know, the whole time we were together, I always felt your heart belonged more to this inn than it did to me."

Instead of trying to explain again how much a part of him Hatteras West was, Alex just smiled and said, "What can I say? She'll always be my first love."

Earnestly, Jenny asked, "Alex, do you honestly believe any woman will accept second place in your heart?"

Alex laughed heartily. "Jenny, if I've learned one thing over the years, it's that anybody I get involved with will have to love Hatteras West almost as much as I do."

Jenny shook her head and smiled softly. "Good luck finding her, Alex, and I mean that sincerely."

Alex caught himself whistling as he walked down the hall to the laundry room. It looked like Jenny had finally accepted the fact that there was nothing but friendship between them, and memories left from their past.

"Why the broad smile?" Emma asked as he walked into the small laundry room. There was a mountain of white cotton sheets in the basket in front of her, and she'd been systematically converting the jumbled mess into a pristinely organized stack.

As Alex grabbed a sheet and started folding, he said, "I'm just happy to be alive today."

"My, you're in a particularly good mood, especially with Elise gone."

"Emma, I can't do anything about that. But this is my home, and there's no place in the world I'd rather be." He chuckled slightly as he put the folded sheet onto the pile and grabbed another one from the basket.

"Alex Winston, sometimes you don't make any sense at all."

He patted her cheek and said, "Just sometimes? Emma, I thought you knew me better than that."

She couldn't help joining him in his laughter; his mood was that infectious. "You're an odd bird, Alex Winston, you know that, don't you?"

"I wouldn't have it any other way."

They were just finishing up the last of the laundry

when Shantara came in. "There you are. I've been looking all over the inn for you."

Alex realized he'd forgotten to put the proper sign on the front desk in case one of his guests needed him. He had a whole batch of ready-made signs telling them where he was, including one that said, I'm in the Laundry Room if You Need Me.

Shantara's eyes, usually so deep and intense, had a very worried look about them.

"What is it?" Alex asked, his good mood suddenly gone.

"It's over, Alex, I can't fake this anymore. I'm canceling what's left of this disaster right now before something else bad happens."

13

"You can't cancel the fair," Alex said. "Shantara, people are counting on you."

She looked ready to burst into tears. "What's the use, Alex? This entire weekend is going to be remembered forever as the Murder Fair."

Alex suddenly felt his blood turn to ice. "Has something happened to Marilynn Baxter?"

Shantara shook her head. "I haven't heard anything about Marilynn. She's probably safe at home by now. I'm talking about Jefferson's murder. Surely that's enough, isn't it?"

Emma said calmly, "Shantara, if you shut the fair down now, whoever killed Jefferson Lee will most likely get away with it. What are the odds the sheriff is going to be able to track down the killer if the majority of his suspects fly the coop? You can't let that happen, not while it's in your hands."

"Mrs. Sturbridge, how can I ask people to pay to see a young blacksmith who may or may not show up, a pottery team who's doubtful, and another blacksmith gone because he was murdered on the spot? The only exhibitors I *know* I can count on are Jenny and Rachel. It's not much of a show with just the two of them."

Emma said, "Shantara, I've told you before, call me Emma, please. You'd better believe all of Elkton Falls will come out here today! If nothing else, they want to see what's going to happen next!" She cut off Shantara's protests with a raised hand. "I'm not saying you should cater to their base desires, but I certainly think you have every right to continue your fair. I, for one, have been looking forward to seeing Jenny Harris do her weaving demonstration this afternoon. Not only that, but I missed Rachel Seabock making a Shaker chair yesterday, and I want to be certain I see it today." She turned to Alex and winked so Shantara couldn't see. "In fact, Alex and I were just discussing that very thing, weren't we?"

"Absolutely," Alex said. "You can't disappoint the people who really care about the old-time crafts. That was one of the reasons you did this, remember?"

"Well," Shantara wavered, but Emma steamed on.

"Tell you what. Why don't I walk around the grounds with you, and we'll make certain everything's ready for the paying guests. You don't mind if I skip out for a few minutes, do you, Alex?"

"Go right ahead. I've got everything here under control."

Alex nodded his approval as the two women left. He had liked Emma Sturbridge from the moment he'd met her as a guest at the inn. There was such an air of confidence about her, a sheer and utter serenity that made him feel that nothing could go wrong whenever she was around.

It was a feeling in great demand lately, and in very

short supply. He'd only met one other person on earth who made him feel that everything would turn out all right, no matter how glum things looked at the time.

And she was currently three hundred miles away.

After Alex finished his early morning chores, it was still too early to start on the rooms, so he decided to catch up with Emma and Shantara and see how the preparations for the last day of the fair were going. He had his own list of things to do for the Lighthouse Lighting ceremony that night, but all that could wait. By the time he got caught up with his day's work once the rooms became available for cleaning, the exhibits would be all packed up and gone.

Jenny was already working at her booth, moving the shuttle back and forth at a furious pace as her feet tapped out different codes on the wooden pedals below her. She could really fly. In front of her, a soft pattern of blues, greens and grays emerged from the yarn. How did she ever manage to keep all those tiny threads of yarn straight? She offered him a quick nod accompanied by a brief smile, then went back to work.

Rachel Seabock was hard at work on a piece of oak wedged securely in her handmade bench that included a clamping vise on one end. She was working the wood with a long, two-handled knife as Alex approached. "Wow, that edge looks sharp," he said as she peeled a curled shaving from the wood.

"It's a drawknife, and it has to be; this oak can be tough to work."

"You're really good at what you do, aren't you?"

Rachel said, "Are you surprised to find a woman working with her hands?" as she jerked the knife through the wood again.

"I'm surprised anybody can master these old tools. My dad taught me woodworking with power tools. I can't imagine doing it all by hand."

"It's different, but to be honest with you, that's why I like it." She slapped her bench and said, "My dad made this shaving horse, but everything else I use is mine. That's how I met Bill in the first place. I needed a new froe, and he made me one out of a car spring." Rachel frowned a moment, then added, "Alex, I'm really worried about him."

Alex looked over at the blacksmith, who was hammering a piece of steel into submission, a scowl plastered on his sweating face. "What's wrong with him?"

"When he didn't show up here last night, I went back to his house and waited for him there. He didn't come home at all, and he won't talk to me this morning. Why can't he see I'm just trying to help?"

Alex had to measure his words carefully. "Rachel, he's a grown man. Maybe he needs to work things out for himself."

"Well, maybe he doesn't know what a good thing he has until he loses it," she said abruptly. "If he doesn't straighten up soon, he's going to find out, because I'm not going to be there for him if he keeps this up."

"Would it help if I talked to him?" The last thing in the world Alex wanted to do was to come between the lovers, but he couldn't stop himself from making the offer.

Rachel considered it a moment, then said, "No, you'd better not say anything to him. No offense, but you'd probably only make things worse."

"If there's anything I can do, let me know."

Alex watched her work the oak blank, drawing the metal across the wood with a sure and steady hand. It amazed him how much raw physical strength a traditional woodworker needed. It was a lot different than flicking on a power tool's switch, and he found a new admiration for someone with the ability to do things the old way.

Alex drifted away as the crowds started to come in and gather around the crafters. Shantara's gatekeeper must have collected the money early in an attempt to stem a rushing tide.

If that was the case, she'd failed miserably. Alex couldn't believe all of the townspeople he saw. Shantara joined him as he watched many of the fair visitors head inexorably for the murder scene, bypassing the few craftspeople actually working.

Shantara came up beside him and said, "You know, the smartest thing I did was to make every day require a different event ticket. I read on the Internet that a lot of organizers offer show passes good for both days, but I didn't want the hassle of another ticket to keep track of. I'm getting people back I never expected to see out here again. At least there aren't any worries about the fair making money."

Alex said, "Shantara, a lot of the people might have come out to see the murder scene, but I'm willing to bet they'll stay for the craft demonstrations since they're already here. Your exhibitors are getting truckloads of new exposure." Before Shantara could cut him off, Alex added, "I hate to see a murder committed here more than you could imagine, but we didn't have anything to do with it. It's no more my fault for rebuilding the Main Keeper's Quarters than it is yours for organizing this fair."

"I suppose you're right, but I've got a confession to make, Alex."

He leaned forward so he wouldn't miss a word. Shantara wrestled with telling him something, then

changed her mind at the last second. Instead of whatever it was she'd been wanting to say, Shantara added
limply, "I'll be glad when this is over."

"Shantara, is there anything you'd like to talk about?
We could go into my office. You know I'm here for
you, don't you?"

She looked tempted for a moment, then said, "I'm
sorry, Alex, there's just no time." Almost whispering,
she added, "It's too late, anyway."

Alex was about to press her further when Bill Yadkin yelled, "Shantara! I need you over here. Now!"

She squeezed Alex's shoulder as she said, "Sorry,
I've got to go."

"We'll talk later," Alex said hopefully.

"Absolutely," she answered with no conviction at all
as she walked away.

Shantara's aborted confession left him troubled.
He'd seen enough of the fair to last him a lifetime.
Now that the exhibitors were into their day, Alex could
work on the rooms, and in the process, perhaps dis-
cover something about what was really going on at
Hatteras West.

Evans Graile was at his usual spot when Alex
walked in. "Morning, Evans. How are you today?"

"I'm ambivalent, my friend. I hate to see the fair
end, it's been such a prime source of entertainment for
me, but I do relish the last few moments of solitude at
Hatteras West before I leave. I'll be checking out tomorrow."

Alex was startled by the news. "I didn't think your
house would be done for another month." Honestly,
with the new construction bills triple what he'd ex-

pected, Alex had been glad for Evans's steady contribution to his financial well-being.

"The house won't be ready, but I'm growing restless here. I thought a European trip might be in order."

It was nearly impossible for Alex to believe that this near shut-in was going on a tour of Europe! "What made you decide to do something so drastic on the spur of the moment?"

Evans stared at his hands as he admitted, "If you must know, it was Jefferson Lee's death."

As Alex started to apologize, Evans said, "No, dear boy, I don't blame you for what happened, not in the least. I didn't sleep at all last night. It finally sank in that someone was actually dead! That young man's murder just showed me that none of us know the number of our days left, and I'm not going to fritter away another minute sitting around watching the world pass me by! No, sir, I've spent enough time on the sidelines to last me the rest of my life."

It was a statement filled with irony, considering the fact that Evans's eyes never left the crowds milling about outside as he spoke.

"Are you going on this trip alone?" Alex asked.

"No, I'm not quite up to that" he admitted. "I've invited my cousin Harry Roberts to go with me. We'll make it a bachelor tour and have a grand old time." Alex knew Harry left the house even less than Evans did. He wondered if the two of them would even leave their hotel room once they arrived in Europe, but he admired their spirit.

"Well, we're going to miss you, Evans, but I hope you two have a wonderful trip."

"I know we shall, Alex. Tell you what, I'll send you a postcard from the Tower of London. I've always wanted to go there, and I'm going to do it before I'm too old to enjoy the experience." He rubbed his hands together vigorously. "And high tea in England! I can hardly wait!"

The world was just full of surprises.

Alex got Elise's cart from the closet upstairs and started toward the first room on his list. He wanted to be certain he was out of Jenny's room before she came back.

Her bags were packed, and her door stood open. Alex was relieved that she was leaving. He'd had a secret fear she'd decide to stay on, and then he wasn't sure what he would do with her. Alex stripped the sheets and cleaned the room, then set everything right again for the next guest. Though he could barely tell the room had been occupied, he still gave it his normal, thorough cleaning. Alex prided himself on running a first-rate inn, something he shared with Elise, and he was determined not to let their high standards slip while she was away.

Rachel's bags were by the door as well, but it was obvious she hadn't even slept in her bed the night before. The towels were still fresh, and the seals in the bathroom were all still in place. She had indeed gone back into town, waiting on Bill Yadkin all night.

When he got to the room Craig and Marilynn shared, he knocked twice before using his passkey to open the door. Alex stood there in the doorway staring at the feminine shape lying motionless on the bed.

After all his earlier searching, he'd found Marilynn Baxter at last.

But was he too late?

14

Alex rushed to the bed. Had the killer struck again? If his pounding on the door hadn't stirred Marilynn, Alex knew she could be in serious trouble. He tried to shake her awake. "Marilynn, are you all right? Marilynn!" As Alex leaned over the bed beside her, he found a prescription bottle, now empty, near one hand.

"Marilynn," he shouted. Her eyelids seemed to flutter for a second before they stopped again. She was still alive!

Alex rushed to the telephone and called Doc Drake's office. He knew Doc usually liked to get an early start on the day.

"He's not here, Alex," Madge the nurse told him. "As a matter of fact, he said he was going to check out the fair before he started work today. I expect he's already out at your place. I'll be glad to beep him if you want."

Alex slammed the phone down before she could say another word.

He tore down the stairs and nearly knocked Evans Graile down. "Evans, go up to room number seven. Marilynn Baxter's overdosed on something."

The man looked shocked by the news. "What can I do for her?"

"Sit with her until I can get Doc Drake," Alex commanded. The older man was startled by Alex's urgent tone, but he hurried up the stairs as Alex ran out onto the front porch.

"Doc! Doc Drake," he called out over the crowd.

The smallish doctor appeared before him as if by magic. He even had his black medical kit with him. "What is it, Alex? Tabby Hilston sprained her ankle, and I promised her I'd take a look at it."

"Marilynn Baxter overdosed on something upstairs."

Doc's face went white. "Which room?"

"Number seven."

As he rushed past Alex, the doctor said, "There's an EMS van at the front gate. Go get them. Alex, do you know what she took?"

"I have no idea," Alex said frantically, "there was a bottle by her hand, but the label's been torn off."

"Okay, I'll handle it. Go get the EMS crew. I'll be upstairs with her."

Alex tore through the crowd, ignoring a dozen hails and greetings. He didn't have time for niceties, not with Marilynn Baxter's life hanging in the balance.

The EMS team, a youngish man and a middle-aged woman, were standing around drinking coffee near the front gate.

"There's an emergency at the inn! The doctor needs you there right now."

Both cups hit the ground as the workers piled into the van.

Alex said, "Cut through the field. You can get to the

back entrance of the inn without running anyone down."

As the emergency rig raced off toward the inn, Tom Lane, the young money collector for the day, grabbed Alex. "What's happened? Is Shantara all right?"

It was obvious the young man had a huge crush on the shopkeeper. "She's fine, Tom. It's one of my guests."

Tom shook his head in wonder. "Man, you surely do have a lot of stuff happen around here don't you, Mr. Winston?"

"More than you can imagine," Alex said as he hurried back to the inn.

The EMS crew was carrying Marilynn out on a stretcher as Alex approached the back porch. There was a clear plastic mask over her face, and Doc Drake was by her side.

"Is she going to be all right?" Alex asked.

Doc shot out, "It's too soon to tell," as he jumped into the back of the vehicle.

With the siren wailing and lights flashing, the EMS van left Hatteras West, racing toward the hospital to save the potter's life.

Evans met Alex at the back door.

Alex said, "Listen, I'm sorry I was so abrupt with you earlier. I didn't mean to snap like that."

"Nonsense, Alex, you did the right thing. I do hope she'll be all right. I'm afraid I wasn't much help up there."

"You were with her, Evans, that's what matters."

"I suppose you're right. Alex, if you don't mind, I think I'll leave the inn a little earlier than I'd planned.

I'd like to check out today if it won't inconvenience you too much."

"I understand how you feel, but where will you stay until your trip?"

Evans grinned slightly. "I'm sure Harry will put me up. To be honest with you, he was a bit miffed when I opted to stay with you instead of him during my renovations. I thought it would be more peaceful here, if you can believe that."

There was nothing Alex could say to that. He couldn't blame Evans Graile a bit.

There was entirely too much excitement at The Hatteras West Inn for his taste, too.

Shantara found Alex a few minutes later. "Alex, did I just see the EMS people leave?"

"Marilynn Baxter just overdosed on something. I found her up in her room while I was cleaning."

Shantara started weeping gently. "Alex, this has turned into the biggest nightmare of my life. Why did I ever start this?"

Alex took her by the shoulders. "Shantara, this isn't your fault. Jefferson Lee would be dead even if there'd never been a Golden Days Fair. Marilynn must have had more problems than any of us realized to try to take her own life like that. You're not to blame for any of it."

His words seemed to soothe her. She hugged him gently, then said, "Oh, Alex, I couldn't have pulled this off without you, and I end up repaying you with nothing but trouble."

He shook his head. "Shantara, you've got to accept that none of this is your fault. By tonight, the fair will be over, and you can start putting it behind you."

"I can't wait," she said. "I feel like I'm taking blood money."

Before Alex could say anything else to calm her, Tabby Hilston limped in, one arm draped around Mor Pendleton's neck.

Mor said, "Alex, did you happen to see Doc Drake? He disappeared on us."

"He had an emergency," Alex explained, not wanting to go into the details of Doc's absence. Tabby didn't look the least put off. In fact, she seemed to enjoy Mor's proximity.

Emma suddenly crashed through the door. "There you are. Mor, I'm sure the lady needs to sit down and take a load off that ankle. There's no need for you to keep supporting her." Emma's face was stern as Mor lowered Tabby into a chair.

Tabby looked unhappy with the new arrangement. She said, "If Doc's not here, how am I going to get to his office? I can't drive with this injury."

She looked expectantly at Mor, but Emma stepped in before he could say a word. "I'll be glad to take you, dear. Mor, would you be so kind as to bring the car around back? I'll have Tabby there when you do, and I can run her into town myself."

"I'd be glad to go with you," Mor said, and Tabby beamed.

Emma wasn't about to give up that easily. "That's sweet of you to offer, but I can handle her all by myself. Why don't you stay here with Alex? We won't be long."

Alex could see Mor clouding up, but the truth was, he really would like his friend's company. "Why don't you hang around, Mor? You can help me change the sheets upstairs."

"Oh, that sounds like pure joy," Mor said, rolling his eyes at Alex.

Emma purposefully ignored the sarcasm. "Good, it's settled then."

Mor knew when he was up against an unmovable force, so he went for his car as Emma had requested. Alex had known his friend too long not to recognize a storm on the horizon between the two of them.

After Tabby was safely loaded into the car and the two women had driven away, Mor followed Alex upstairs.

As Alex stripped Marilynn Baxter's bed, Mor said, "Why do some women get so possessive, Alex? It's not like Emma and I have anything exclusive going on. Sure, we have a great time together, she's a wonderful woman, but my word, I can't even talk to another woman without looking over my shoulder first. It's worse than being married."

Alex said, "If you're asking for my advice about women, you're talking to the wrong man. I don't have a clue."

Mor started laughing in agreement. "We're a real pair, my friend. Have you heard from Elise today?"

"No, but that's understandable. Her father's undergoing surgery today, so I don't expect to hear from her anytime soon."

Mor, in a rare serious mood, said, "You really miss her, don't you?"

"More than I probably should," Alex said as he spread the new sheets out on the bed. Despite his earlier theatrical objections, Mor helped him tuck the corners in.

"So why don't you get off your duff and do something about it?" Mor suggested.

"It's not that simple. She's got a fiancé, remember? In fact, she's with him right now."

"They're engaged, Alex, they're not married. If you ask me, there's a world of difference between the two."

"I don't know," Alex said.

They were just finishing the room when Craig Monroe burst in. His face was white with shock. "Is it true? Is Marilynn dead?"

Alex said, "Craig, she's still alive. In fact, she should be at the hospital by now. I looked for you at your booth to tell you I'd found her, but you weren't there."

Was there an instant of surprise on Craig's face when Alex told him his wife was still alive? Alex wasn't sure, it had flashed past so quickly.

"I was still out searching for her. I've got to get over there," Craig said, rushing back out the door.

Alex called out, "Do you want one of us to drive you?" but Craig was already gone.

"Now what do you make of that?" Alex asked.

"He's pretty upset, but he's got every right to be, doesn't he? It doesn't speak well of his marriage when his wife tries to commit suicide."

Alex said, "Did you see the look on his face the instant I told him she was still alive?"

"What are you getting at?" Mor asked.

"I could swear the only thing that surprised him was the fact that she wasn't dead."

Mor patted Alex's shoulder. "My friend, your over-active imagination is at work again. The guy's in shock. Give him a break."

"I guess you're right. I probably read it wrong."

Mor sighed. "But you don't think so for a second, do you?"

Alex didn't answer. Had he truly seen what he thought he had, or was Mor right? One thing was certain. He'd feel a great deal better once Marilynn was conscious again and could tell them if she'd really tried to kill herself, or if someone had goaded her into it.

15

The evening came at last, and the Golden Days Fair was officially history. Shantara stood on the steps leading into the lighthouse and used it as an impromptu stage as dusk started to fall. She had planned all along to announce the end of the festival by holding the giveaway drawings visitors had registered for when they'd bought their tickets at the gate, and Alex had convinced her that she needed to follow it through all the way to the end.

Alex walked out onto the front porch in an effort to block anyone from coming into the inn as much as to watch the prize drawings. He'd had his fill of walk-ins, and he didn't care how much future business he might lose by turning people away.

Each of the crafters had donated one item from their wares for the drawings. On the first day of the fair, Alex had bought a ticket himself, though Shantara had scolded him for doing it. It was hard to believe now, looking at the crowd gathered there, but he'd actually been afraid Shantara wouldn't even make back her expenses.

"Thanks for coming," she said to the crowd as they settled down. "We've all seen some wonderful artisans at work over the past two days, and our giveaways are a testimony to their skills. I'd like us all to observe a moment of silence for Jefferson Lee before we announce the prizewinners."

The crowd quieted, and Alex could hear the whispering of the wind through the trees near the lighthouse. After a few seconds, Shantara looked up and said, "Thank you. Now let's get right to the prizes. First up is this wonderful handmade piece by Jenny Harris." Shantara held up Jenny's contribution, a shawl sparkling with velvet blues and purples.

Shantara reached down into a barrel holding all of the entry tickets and announced, "The winner of this lovely shawl is . . . Mor Pendleton."

There were wild hoots from the audience as Mor stepped forward to collect his prize. It looked to Alex like his friend regretted having entered the drawing as he collected the shawl and hastily made his way back into the crowd.

Next she held up a beautiful oak chair Rachel had created. It was the real reason Alex had even entered his ticket into the drawing. He could just barely afford one of Rachel's pieces, but Alex couldn't justify spending the money to buy one for himself, not with the costs of the new construction going higher and higher.

"And the winner is . . . Travis Jenks." Alex recognized one of the kids from Shantara's cleanup crew go to the steps to collect his prize. He held the chair up over his head and shouted to his crowd of friends standing nearby.

The donated pottery tea set went to an older woman

Alex didn't recognize, while Bill Yadkin's iron napkin rings went to a woman from town named Ruby Garnet.

Alex thought the drawings were over when Shantara announced, "We have one last item to give away, contributed by Jefferson Lee."

As the crowd quieted, Alex looked out over the people gathered there. Many of them had come to see the murder scene as well as the festival, and Alex could feel an undercurrent buzz in the air.

Shantara broke the silence by holding up a delicately formed leafy vine a foot long that Jefferson had created out of steel. No matter what the world had thought of the man, he truly had been an artist with iron and fire.

Shantara reached into the barrel and drew out a name. "I'm pleased to announce that the winner is none other than our host, Alex Winston."

There were a few disappointed groans under the cheers as Alex stepped forward to receive his prize. The work was even lovelier up close. As he took the vine from Shantara, Alex could see the veins on the leaves etched into the iron.

He faded back as quickly as he could, clutching the prize in one hand.

Shantara said, "I want to thank you all for coming and making this fair a success. Feel free to stay for the Lighthouse Lighting, and be sure to have a safe drive home."

As the visitors made their way back to their cars to retrieve blankets and picnic baskets for the ceremony, the craftspeople began breaking down their sites. In less than twenty minutes, all that was left was Jefferson Lee's forge standing alone in one corner of the yard and the potters' booth in another. Alex found Shantara packing up the pottery exhibit, wrapping everything carefully.

"Why don't you let that wait," Alex said. "It's almost time for the lighting." He grinned. "Besides, I'll help you do this after everyone else is gone."

"I can't ask you to do that, Alex, you've done so much already." She pointed to the kids working around her. "Besides, I can't just bug out and leave them all here to finish without me."

"They're not going to take off without you, Shantara. You're buying the pizza, remember?" Alex grabbed her hand. "Come on, you can climb the steps with me."

"Can I throw the switch?"

"Don't push it," he said, laughing.

The interior of the lighthouse was dark as Alex and Shantara climbed the steps together, a single flashlight between them. By the time they got to the observation deck, the crowd had settled in, ready for the ceremony.

Alex called out to the people below, "We light this torch for those who have gone before, from the brave men and women who were the first keepers of the flame to all our comrades and loved ones who have fallen since."

With that, he ducked inside and pressed the ordinary-looking black button that controlled the Fresnel lens. In a moment, the light came on and began to slowly rotate, shining out into the night around them.

Alex could hear the mass of cheers from below. Normally, he loved the ceremony, an event that occurred once a year when he could light the beacon with the local government's blessing.

It just wasn't the same this year, whether because of the recent murder, the Golden Days Fair, or, he had to admit to himself, the fact that Elise was gone.

"It's awfully bright up here," Shantara said. "How long are you going to keep the lens on?"

"I always give it thirty minutes, rain or shine. Let's go back down and enjoy the festivities. I think we both need a break."

Alex and Shantara split up as they walked among the blankets filled with families of all sizes and shapes. There were greetings from old friends and new ones as kids of all ages watched the light rotate into the night, mesmerized. It really was quite a sight; Alex had to admit it. He never got tired of seeing Hatteras West in all its glory, its beacon shining brightly; he only wished the town council would ease up on their restrictions and let him fire up the Fresnel lens more often.

But for now, for that moment at that place and time, all was well with Alex's world as the beacon completed another turn into the darkness.

Once the light was shut off for another year and the crowds were all gone, Alex followed Shantara back to the demonstration area. Temporary floodlights lit the area showing a lawn picked clean of debris. The two exhibits still standing were the only signs that the Golden Days Fair had ever been there.

As she started to work at packing up the display, Shantara said, "You really don't have to help, Alex, I can take care of this myself."

"I know I don't have to," Alex said as he grabbed a stack of newspapers and started wrapping pottery pieces. "To be honest with you, I'm so keyed up from lighting the lens that I won't get to sleep for hours, anyway."

"Okay, then, I give up."

As they worked, he said, "So what happened to all the kids? I can't believe they left without you."

"I told them they could go. I called Irma, and she's started the pizzas." She wiped her forehead. "Besides, I just want to go home, take a good long soak and forget about the world for a while."

They worked well together, storing and stacking the pottery and equipment left behind.

Alex looked over at the murder victim's exhibit and said, "What's going to happen to Jefferson's exhibit?"

"Bill Yadkin's agreed to take it down for me as soon as he gets his own display back to his shop." She glanced at her watch. "It's getting late, though. Alex, do you mind if it stays up until tomorrow?"

"It's fine with me," Alex said, though the last thing in the world he wanted was a reminder of the slain blacksmith.

Shantara said, "Bill's thinking about making a bid on the equipment from whoever ends up with Jefferson's estate."

"I can't believe he'd want it, not after the feud the two of them had."

Shantara shrugged as she secured the lid to the final box. "He says good equipment is hard to come by, and he doesn't want the tools to just go on display somewhere. The anvil alone is supposed to be some kind of real prize for collectors, but Bill wants to keep it to use."

"So what are you going to do with all of this?" Alex asked, gesturing to the pile of filled boxes.

"I'm keeping everything at the store until Craig can pick it all up. Have you heard anything about Marilynn?"

"The last I heard, she was still unconscious." Alex

didn't add his own suspicions of Craig Monroe's reaction. Shantara had enough troubles on her mind.

Shantara nodded. "I don't care how late it is, I'm changing my plans and going by the hospital as soon as we're done." She surveyed their work and said, "Thanks for helping, Alex. You'll have your inn back in no time." Her expression turned serious as she added "Are you sure I can't pay you rent for the use of Hatteras West? I've suddenly found myself with more profit than I ever could have imagined. Don't worry," she added quickly, "I'm paying Jefferson's heirs every dime I owed him, but with all the extra traffic, I still made out pretty well."

"Put it back for a rainy day, Shantara. You don't owe me a thing."

Shantara kissed Alex on the cheek, and Alex noticed that one of the workers he'd met earlier, Tom Lane, was watching them closely from the shadows.

As he stepped out of the darkness into the light, Tom looked quickly away, but not before Alex saw the young man's burning cheeks.

Alex said, "Don't look now, but I think you've got an admirer."

Shantara turned and saw Tom watching them. He smiled gently at her as he moved toward them. "Tom's had a crush on me since he was twelve. He's still just a boy, Alex."

"Don't tell him that. He's in his early twenties, isn't he?"

Shantara shrugged. "Something like that, but he's still too young for me."

Alex smiled. "Don't be so sure. Look at Bill and Rachel."

Shantara laughed. "That's not the greatest example in the world, now, is it? We both know how well that's working out, don't we? No thanks, I think I'll stick to men my own age."

Alex said, "That's really cutting down on the dating pool around Elkton Falls, isn't it? You might have to go back to your first boyfriend and start the cycle all over again."

Shantara's laughter was infectious. "No thank you, he's as round as a basketball and as bald as a rock." She sighed heavily and added, "Alex, I swear I'm going to sleep for a week, and I'm starting tonight."

Tom made it a point to approach them. His voice was stilted and formal as he asked, "Where would you like these boxes?"

"Why don't you bring your truck over here, Tom, and we can load all this up. If you don't mind the extra work, you can help me haul everything back to my store. I'd be happy to pay you extra."

"You don't have to, Shantara, I don't mind helping," he muttered as he turned his back on them and walked off.

"Now what was that all about?" Shantara asked. "He's never acted that way around me before."

"He thinks we were laughing at him instead of each other," Alex said.

"Oh, my, I just hate ruffled feathers. Excuse me, Alex, I'd better go talk to him."

He saw the two of them in deep conversation, then after a few minutes, Tom walked quickly to his truck with a new spring in his step as Shantara rejoined Alex.

"Whatever you said to him, it surely worked," Alex said.

"Alex Winston, if you give me grief about this, I swear I'll never forgive you."

"What did I say?" Alex asked innocently.

"It's not what you said, it's what you're going to say

when I tell you I'm having dinner with Tom tomorrow night. I'm still not sure how it happened."

Alex smiled at her. "I'm just going to say one thing, then I promise I'll shut up."

Shantara's nose crinkled as she said, "Go ahead. I suppose I deserve it."

"I hope you two have a nice time," Alex said as he walked back to the inn alone.

The phone was ringing as Alex hurried back inside. It was late for anyone who knew him to be calling, but Alex hoped there was word about Marilynn's condition.

It took him a second to realize it was Elise on the other end of the phone as she said, "I was about ready to give up on you. I've tried calling three times already this evening."

"I'm sorry, Elise. I've been away from the desk, and I forgot to put the answering machine on with everything that's been going on around here. How's your father doing?"

"He came out of surgery a few hours ago. Everything went better than they expected. The doctor seems to think he'll be out of here in no time."

The relief in her voice was obvious.

"I'm so happy for you," Alex said.

"So, what's been happening there?" she asked.

For a moment Alex considered postponing telling her about Marilynn Baxter's attempted suicide, but he knew Elise would be furious if she found out he'd been holding back on her.

"Elise, I found Marilynn Baxter in her room today. She'd taken an overdose of something."

"Is she . . . dead?"

"The last I heard, she's still unconscious, but I admit I haven't spoken with Doc Drake in a while. It was a good thing he was already out at the fair. I think it might have saved her life."

"It sounds to me like it was a good thing for Marilynn that you were there yourself. How did you happen to find her?"

"I was cleaning the rooms," Alex admitted.

"Oh, Alex, isn't Emma helping you at all?"

He said, "Absolutely. You know how crazy things can get around here, even without a fair. We've had our hands full, what with the Lighthouse Lighting tonight."

"I forgot all about that being tonight. How was it, Alex?"

"It was wonderful. I wish you could have seen it yourself."

"Me, too." Her words were followed by a momentary awkward silence on the line.

Alex filled it by gently asking, "When are you coming back?"

Instead of answering his question, Elise said hurriedly, "Alex, I've got to go. The doctor just came out of the Cardiac Intensive Care Unit, and he's talking to Mom."

Alex said, "Good-bye," but the line was already dead.

He couldn't help wondering if the doctor really had shown up or if Elise had just used it as an excuse to sidestep his question. Like it or not, he was going to have to deal with the possibility that Elise might not be coming back to Hatteras West ever again.

It looked like Alex might have to face the fact that Elise wasn't going to be a part of his life anymore.

16

Late the next morning, Alex had just finished dust-mopping the floor when Mor came in. "Hey, Alex, is Emma around?"

"To be honest with you, I forgot she was supposed to be coming back today. I haven't seen her all morning." He smiled at Mor as he added, "I've just about got the inn clean, so your timing's perfect."

Mor smiled. "That's the best news I've heard all day. I didn't want to spend my day off cleaning rooms with you again, not that it wasn't a real treat before." He pointed to a stack of luggage by the front desk. "What are all those bags doing there?"

"Just about everything there belongs to Craig and Marilynn." He pointed to a single black overnight bag. "That one belonged to Jefferson Lee. I'm dropping it off at the police station for the sheriff."

Mor looked around the lobby, and when he saw it was deserted, he asked, "Where's your resident snoop? Evans isn't actually out in the real world, is he?"

Alex laughed. "You're not going to believe this. He's taking a tour of Europe with Harry Roberts. He's over there right now planning it all."

Mor said, "I've seen everything now. Les isn't going to believe me when I tell him tomorrow." Les was the older part of the partnership of Mor or Les. The two handymen kept most of Elkton Falls running while forming a deep friendship, though neither man would admit it under knifepoint.

Mor nudged Jefferson's bag with his toe. "So, what did you find in there? Were there any clues?"

"I don't know what you're talking about," Alex said as innocently as he could manage. "It's just his clothes and toiletries."

"Don't play that game with me, bucko. I know you're not about to let a perfectly good opportunity to snoop get past you."

Alex shrugged in admission. "For all the good it did me. That man barely made an impression on the room. It was almost as if a ghost had stayed there."

Mor said, "Maybe you've got one around here now. Have you given that any thought?"

"What are you jabbering about, Mor?"

The big man had an odd expression on his face. "You know what they say, Alex. Ghosts hang around after a violent death, and getting skewered is about as violent as it gets."

Alex snorted at his friend's serious tone. "Who knows? Maybe a ghost or two will help business. I can put it in my brochures."

Mor laughed. "Alex, you're an innkeeper through and through, aren't you?"

"It's in my blood. Listen, do you have anything pressing planned for today?"

"No, this is the last place on my list to look for Emma. I'm not sure what to do now."

Alex asked, "How would you like to do me a favor, then?"

"What's the matter, does the septic system need to be cleaned out?"

"No, this is easy. Hang around here a couple of hours by the front desk and answer the telephone for me. My guests are all gone now that the crafters have left, and the next group isn't scheduled until tomorrow, but I'm expecting a call from a travel agent who's promised to book the entire inn for a full week this autumn."

"Why can't you put your answering machine on for that?"

"Because she's not going to want to use Hatteras West if she thinks I'm an absentee innkeeper. Listen, if it's a problem, I'll hang around myself."

Mor picked up a magazine and said, "No, I'll take care of it. I need to have a talk with Emma anyway, and she's as likely to show up here as anywhere I could look."

Alex wasn't about to open that hornet's nest if he could help it. "Thanks, man, you're the best. I'll be back in a few hours."

After Alex loaded all of the luggage in the cab of his old gray Ford pickup, he drove toward town, glancing back at the lighthouse as he went. The structure stood there as a constant, a landmark in his life, always watching over him. Somehow its presence made him feel safe. Too bad it hadn't helped Jefferson Lee or Marilynn Baxter.

• • •

Alex's first stop was the hospital. He wanted to check on Marilynn's condition, and the luggage he was carrying would give him the perfect excuse to be there.

He asked a volunteer at the front desk wearing a name tag that said Bob about Marilynn. The man tapped a few keys on the computer and directed him to the Intensive Care Unit.

Alex found Craig Monroe there looking a hundred years older than he had the day before. Was it worry or guilt that had aged him overnight?

"How's she doing?" Alex asked.

Craig looked surprised by his presence, lost in his own thoughts. "No change. Alex, I've been meaning to ask you, what were you doing up in our room, anyway? Not that I'm not grateful," he added hastily.

"I was doing my daily cleaning. When no one answered my knock, I used my passkey."

Craig pushed. "Alex, did she say anything at all the whole time you were there?"

What an odd question! Alex was just about to answer when he saw Sheriff Armstrong strolling down the hallway. "Hey there, Alex. Got a second?"

"Hang on, Sheriff, I'll be right with you." He turned back to Craig. "I've got your bags with me in my truck. Where would you like them?"

The potter said, "Why don't we head over to my house together, and you can help me carry everything inside."

"Don't you need to be here with your wife?" Alex asked pointedly.

"Yeah, I suppose you're right. Alex, I still need to talk to you later."

"Not a problem," Alex said as he walked down the hall with Armstrong. There had been an edge and an urgency to Monroe's request that Alex didn't like. He promised himself that if he did have another talk with the potter, he was going to make darn sure it was in a well-lit place with lots of other people around.

Alex asked Armstrong, "Are you here investigating what happened to Marilynn Baxter?"

The sheriff shook his head. "Nope. From what I hear, there's nothing to investigate. She tried to kill herself. Whether she succeeds or not is still up in the air. I had to swing by the hospital to check on a drunk driver from NewCon. Some guy got a snoot full, then decided to go joyriding in Elkton Falls. Why he didn't stay there and be Dave Wooster's headache, I'll never know."

"I don't know how to put this, but I'm not so sure Marilynn Baxter tried to kill herself."

Armstrong grabbed Alex's arm and led him to an al-cove nearby. "Alex, do you have any facts to back up that wild talk?"

"Nothing for sure." He hesitated telling the sheriff that his gut reacted strongly to Craig Monroe's attitude about his wife.

The sheriff grimaced. "Alex, don't go spreading this around Elkton Falls. I've got enough trouble on my hands without you adding to it. I understand the lady's been depressed lately. It happens more often than you and I would ever imagine."

"Where did you hear that she was depressed?" Alex asked.

"Why, her husband told me himself. He would know if anybody would, don't you think? After all, he lived with the woman."

Not exactly a reliable source at the moment, Alex thought to himself. Before he could voice his suspicions that Craig Monroe might have had something a little more active to do with his wife's current condition, the sheriff said, "Alex, I've seen that look in your eyes before. Drop this, you hear me? If you want something to do, I'll try to find it for you, but leave this one alone."

Alex decided to change tactics. "Have you had any luck solving Jefferson Lee's murder?"

"I'm close to an arrest; that's all I'll say." The smug look on the sheriff's face was too much for Alex. "I'll grant you this, you were right about the postcard. I'm almost positive it was connected to the murder."

"Come on, Sheriff, you've got to tell me more than that. Who do you think did it?"

"You'll find out when the rest of Elkton Falls does, Alex. I'm not about to say anything and have my suspect get wind of it before I can make my arrest." He held up his hands. "Not that I don't trust you, but these walls have ears, if you know what I mean."

Alex suddenly remembered the blacksmith's bag in his truck. "Sheriff, I've got Jefferson Lee's things from the inn. I was going to run them by your office, but you can get them now, if you'd like."

"I've already been through all of it, Alex." The sheriff scratched his chin, then said, "Tell you what. It couldn't hurt to check them out again, so why don't we walk out together, and I'll have another look. Who knows, there might be something that will help my case."

After the sheriff had gone through Jefferson's bag outside, he said, "I just don't get it, Alex. His house is the same way. You can barely find a personal thing in the whole place. I mean it was creepy. There were no photographs, no collections on display, the man barely made a dent in his own home. I just can't imagine living like that."

"So, what happens now?"

"I'll take this bag over to his house." The sheriff suddenly had a thought. "Hey, you have a few minutes to spare?"

Alex knew he shouldn't impose on Mor any more than he had to, but he was intrigued enough to ask, "What did you have in mind?"

"I thought I'd give you a gander at the man's house and see what you thought yourself. Strictly unofficial, if you follow me."

"Let's go," Alex said eagerly. Maybe he could find something the sheriff and his team had missed.

For once Armstrong hadn't exaggerated. Jefferson Lee had barely made an impression on his living space. It seemed as if the entire set of furnishings had been ordered from one catalogue, perfectly matched and co-ordinated. All the proper shades of color and tone blended together until there wasn't the slightest personal touch or originality in the whole place. Alex wondered if the man's workshop was the same as the house, and he started to ask the sheriff if he could peek inside the outbuilding as well, when a sudden squawk came from the sheriff's beeper.

Armstrong checked the number, then called his dispatcher on Jefferson's telephone.

"Yeah, you just paged me. What's up?"

There was a pause, then he said, "I'll be right there."

"What happened?" Alex asked as the sheriff hung up the phone.

"There's a wreck out on Highway 127. Some joker with a Jet Ski on his trailer was headed for the lake, and it slipped off the back end. Smacked right into a hearse, and now nobody can get through. I need to head out there pronto. Listen Alex, I hate to do this to you, but can you get back to the hospital on your own? It's a good four miles out of my way, and they need me out there right now."

"I'll be fine," Alex said. "Do you want me to lock up when I'm done here?"

Armstrong looked as if he'd assumed Alex would leave with him, but he was obviously in too big a hurry to stand there and debate the fact with him.

"Just pull the door shut when you're done, and don't let anybody else in, okay?"

Alex agreed, and as the sheriff headed for the door, he added, "Alex, if you find anything, you call my office right away, you understand?"

"I promise," Alex said as the sheriff took off.

Now maybe he could do a little snooping of his own.

An hour later, Alex was no closer to finding anything inside Jefferson's house than he had been when he'd first come in. How in blazes could the man live like that? Alex only hoped the shop would yield something, any clue as to why Jefferson Lee was murdered.

The key to Jefferson's shop hung on a Shaker peg by the doorway. Alex knew the blacksmith's building, with its roaring fires and blackened soot, had to be separate from the house, and he was glad he'd spotted the neatly labeled key as he walked back to the modern shop.

It turned out that Alex hadn't needed the key, after all.

Someone had beaten him to the search, and from the look of the place, they hadn't been too careful disguising their presence there. He was certain the sheriff would never have wrecked the shop in his investigation, nor would he have left it like that without saying something to Alex about it.

As Alex headed back inside to phone the sheriff's office, he wondered if the thief had found what he'd been looking for.

17

Alex called the sheriff's office and spoke with one of Armstrong's deputies, a young man named Dave Jeffries. Alex had known Dave all of his life. He'd been coming out to the lighthouse with his family since he was a small boy, and he'd always tried to convince Alex to light the beacon for him, even if he was visiting at high noon.

The deputy asked him to hang around until he could get there, and Alex readily agreed.

After he hung up the phone, Alex walked back to the shop to have a look around before Dave arrived.

Instead of the old-fashioned equipment Alex had been expecting to see in the shop, he found huge steel machines outfitted with wicked-looking attachments spread all through the blacksmith's shop. It appeared that the quaint equipment Jefferson had set up at the fair had been more for the exhibition than for his daily work. Alex wasn't all that surprised.

The floor of the shop was littered with a thousand

papers. Was there a key in all that mess to Jefferson's murder, or had the killer taken a piece of evidence after disposing of the man himself? Alex saw bills, plans, even correspondence with other blacksmiths discussing things like power hammers and a host of other topics Alex didn't understand, but nothing that might point to the murderer.

"Find anything good in there?"

Alex didn't know how long he'd been looking, but he was startled to hear the voice. He looked up from his squatting position to see the young deputy standing in the doorway. There was a smile on Dave's narrow face and an easy way about him that Alex had always liked. Armstrong's uniform was in constant need of expansion, but Dave's was as neat and tailored as the day he'd first put it on.

"Hey, Dave. I was just—"

"Snooping again, Alex? Hey, I'm not the one in our department who has a problem with that. As far as I'm concerned, you can look all you want, as long as that's all you do." He looked at the papers strewn on the floor. "Now that is one major mess. You didn't touch anything, did you?"

Alex shook his head. "I know better than that. I've just been doing some light reading."

Dave stroked his chin. "I wonder if they found what they were looking for."

"I was just thinking the same thing."

The deputy said, "Alex, thanks for calling this in, but you'd better take off. I talked to the sheriff on the way over here, and he's heading back just as soon as he can clear up that accident." Dave grinned. "From the sound of it, he's a little unhappy that you found this break-in instead of him. It wouldn't hurt to keep a low profile for the next few hours, if you know what I mean."

Alex nodded. "Thanks. I just have to use the phone inside; then I'll take off."

"I'll be right here," the deputy said, still staring at the mess on the floor.

Alex needed to telephone the inn. He felt a little uneasy using the dead man's phone, as if he were intruding. It was the oddest feeling.

It took seven rings before Mor finally picked up.

Alex said, "I almost gave up on you."

"This isn't a great time, Alex. Emma and I are in the middle of something."

Alex didn't want to know any of the details. He had enough on his plate as it was.

"Did that travel agent phone?" he asked quickly.

"No, you're the first call I've had. Listen, take your time getting back. It looks like we're going to be a while."

Alex hung up, forgetting for a moment that he'd called Mor with the intent of getting a ride back to his truck.

That was out of the question now. His stomach growled, and Alex realized he'd skipped lunch again. It wasn't that he wasn't hungry, but he'd grown accustomed to eating with Elise at the inn, and without her to remind him, Alex had a tendency to work right through the noonday meal.

Buck's Grill was close enough to walk to, and after grabbing a bite to eat, Alex was fairly certain he'd be able to find someone to give him a lift back to his truck. It was the other side of the coin to small town life. Everybody always seemed to know everybody else's business, but they were also willing to help out at the drop of a hat when they were needed.

It was one of the many pluses that made the few minuses worthwhile.

The crowd at Buck's had thinned considerably, and Alex didn't have any trouble grabbing a seat at the counter. Elise always liked to sit in a booth when they ate at the diner, but Alex liked to be near the griddle, where the action was. In all honesty, he kind of missed the playful debate with her about where to sit.

Buck's daughter Sally Anne was wiping the counter as Alex sat down. Instead of the typical teasing he normally got from her, Sally Anne gave him a sympathetic smile as she put a large glass of iced tea in front of him and quickly filled a small pitcher with more of the same.

"Would you like your usual?" she asked softly.

Alex nodded. "How about some extra fries with that today? I'm really hungry."

She nodded, scribbled his order on her pad, then called out to her father in back, "Dad, order up."

She took her rag and cleaned the spot just beside him, one that was already gleaming. "Alex, I'm so sorry. You must be crushed."

He finished a sip of the wonderful sweet tea and said, "I hate to see anyone murdered, but if it had to happen, I'd rather it wasn't at Hatteras West."

"I'm not talking about the murder, Alex; that's old news. It's got to be hard, what with Elise packing up and leaving you in the middle of all this mess."

"Sally Anne, she's visiting family. There was a medical emergency."

The young waitress nodded knowingly. "I understand, Alex. Listen, you've always been a good friend to me. If you need to talk or anything, give me a call, okay?"

Though her sentiment was misplaced, Sally Anne did have a good heart. Besides, he was tired of denying the rumors.

"Thanks, Sally Anne, I'll keep that in mind."

She patted his hand and smiled softly. "You do that, Alex. I'm here for you if you need me."

The bell in the kitchen rang, and in a moment Alex found his club sandwich in front of him. Buck had really laid on the fries, and Alex dove in.

Buck came out as Alex took the second bite of his sandwich.

"How goes it, Alex?" he asked in a gruff voice that matched his muscular frame.

Buck was a former Golden Gloves boxing champion, with the meaty build and broken nose to prove it. When he spoke, it was always more of a growl than mere words.

"I'm fine, Buck. I saw you out running the other day. You can really move."

"For a guy my age and my size, you mean? I'm in training," he said with a grin.

"You're going to fight again?" Alex asked incredulously.

Buck said, "No, I've got something more important than that coming up." He looked at his daughter, then asked, "Can I at least tell him? Alex knows how to keep his mouth shut."

"Dad, we're not telling anybody yet. You know that."

Whatever they were discussing, Alex certainly was intrigued. Buck looked around the diner. "Nobody can hear us. Go on, tell him."

"I'm getting married," she said softly.

"Congratulations," Alex said. "Eric's a lucky man."

Sally Anne said, "Alex, I'm sorry about the timing and all. I was going to tell you later."

Buck put a meaty paw on Alex's shoulder. "He's a strong man, Sally Anne, there's no need to tiptoe around him. Go on, ask him now."

Sally Anne said, "We were wondering if we could get married at the inn. Alex, it's such a beautiful place, and you know how much I've always loved the lighthouse. You don't have to decide now; the wedding's not for another six months. I just wanted to ask," she tapered her words down to a near whisper at the end.

"I don't need to think about it. I'd be delighted to have your wedding at Hatteras West."

Buck lightly slapped his daughter with the towel that was always parked over his shoulder. "See? I told you there was nothing to worry about. I've got to get back to the kitchen." He patted Alex's arm again. "Thanks. This means a lot to us."

"Happy to do it," Alex said as he turned back to his sandwich. The Hatteras West Inn was a perfect place for a wedding, and several townspeople had held their nuptials there. His own mother and father had even married on the grounds, though they'd exchanged their vows from the very top of the lighthouse, something that hadn't been repeated since. It had severely limited the number of invited guests, and Alex's mother had always said that had been his father's main reason for making the request. Alex knew the truth, though. The lighthouse had been as much a part of his dad as it was of him. The Winston men were part of a long line of hopeless romantics, from the lighthouse's builder all the way down to Alex.

Yes, another wedding would be perfect for Hatteras

West. Alex would never have admitted it to anyone else, but he was already looking forward to it.

He was just finishing his meal when Sandra walked in, a harried look on her face.

Sandra smiled quickly the moment she saw Alex. "Hey there, stranger. How are things at the inn?"

"With the fair over, I'm expecting things to finally slow down."

She put her briefcase down on the counter, then slipped onto the stool beside him. Whatever her faults, Sandra almost always found a way to make him smile. "Please tell me you're at least having a piece of pie for dessert. I hate to eat alone."

"Sandra, I left Mor in charge of the inn three hours ago. I really should be getting back."

"Come on, Alex," she said, touching his arm lightly. "Your guests are all gone, and you've got to be done with your cleaning for the day. I know you too well. Keep me company. I hate to eat alone."

Sally Anne was watching the exchange with interest, standing just close enough not to miss a word.

Alex nodded as he finished another fry. "Okay, on one condition. I need a ride to the hospital after we're done here."

"Oh, Alex, what's wrong?"

"I'm fine," he said, "but I left my truck in the parking lot."

Clearly she wanted to know why he'd done that, but remarkably, Sandra didn't ask. "It's a deal."

Sally Anne stepped forward, and Sandra said, "I'll have my regular salad and an iced tea. And bring Alex a piece of apple pie."

Sally Anne took the order without a word, and Alex wondered if she approved entirely of his sharing counter space with his ex-girlfriend.

Sandra took a long drink of tea, then asked, "So tell me, Alex, how's your impromptu investigation doing? Have you uncovered the killer yet?"

Alex said, "What makes you think I'm trying to do anything about the murder?"

She laughed brightly. "Oh, come on, Alex, don't forget who you're talking to. I know how much you love a good mystery."

"Right now I'm just trying to keep my head above water. I don't have much time for sleuthing."

Sally Anne quietly slipped their food in front of them, and Sandra took a few bites of her salad before replying. "Well, I don't think Bill Yadkin did it, for what it's worth, though Armstrong appears to be favoring him. That boy's temper is going to get him into some serious trouble if he's not careful. He fired me, you know."

"Why in the world did he do that?" Alex asked.

"I have no idea, but he'd better hire someone else fast; Armstrong's baying at the door."

Alex had to admit he enjoyed sharing the time with Sandra. The new friendship building between them was nice, devoid of the tension they'd shared while dating.

But she wasn't Elise.

Sandra didn't reach for Alex's check as she grabbed hers, something she'd always done when they'd dated. It had underscored how much more she made as a successful lawyer than he did as an innkeeper, and it had bothered him more than he cared to admit.

"Come on, pay your check and let's go. I've got the top down on my convertible," Sandra said as she headed for the door.

"Are you sure you have to go straight back to the hospital? It's a beautiful afternoon for a drive."

"Sorry, Sandra, but I need to get back." Instead of arguing, she pulled into the hospital parking lot and headed straight for Alex's truck. The gray Ford was hard to miss.

She stopped in front of his spot, and Alex hopped out. "Thanks for the ride, Sandra."

She smiled broadly at him. "You're very welcome. Thanks for keeping me company. Call me, Alex. Any time. No strings, no ulterior motives."

As she sped away, Alex suddenly felt someone else's presence nearby.

He normally wasn't all that jumpy, but as Alex got his car keys out, he felt a tap on his shoulder and promptly dropped his keys on the ground.

When he turned around, the last person on earth he wanted to see was standing right behind him.

18

Craig Monroe leaned over and scooped up Alex's keys before he could grab them himself. Instead of giving them back, Craig enveloped them in his meaty fist. The potter's strong hands reminded Alex that he'd easily have the strength to dispatch Jefferson Lee.

"There you are. I was beginning to wonder if you were ever coming back."

Alex's eyes scanned the parking lot for some kind of witness, but it was remarkably deserted for that time of day.

"How's Marilynn doing?"

"Still no change," Craig grunted. "Alex, I need to talk to you."

"I'm listening," Alex said warily.

Craig shook his head. "Not here, it's a little too public."

What was he talking about? The parking lot was practically abandoned.

"Craig, I've got an inn to run. I'm late as it is, and

Mor's relieving me at the desk. Can I have my keys? I need to go."

Craig looked surprised that he still had Alex's keys locked in his fist. He gave them to Alex as he said, "Can I come out to Hatteras West later? It's important."

"Okay," Alex said. Anything to get out of the parking lot. "See you later."

At least he'd have a chance to prepare for the encounter, and Hatteras West was his own turf. Alex suddenly had a flash of inspiration. He'd get Mor to hang around and back him up, just in case.

When Alex walked back into the inn, Mor was alone at the desk, looking glum.

"You look like you just lost your best friend," Alex said.

Instead of the playful retort he expected, Mor muttered, "I don't want to talk about it." He stood and grabbed his jacket. "If you don't need me here anymore, I'm getting hungry."

Alex said, "To be honest with you, I was kind of hoping you'd be able to hang around. I'm sure I can find something for you in the refrigerator."

"Sorry, but I've got to hit the road."

Alex said, "Any chance of you coming back later?" He suddenly felt awkward, asking Mor to hang around to protect him.

"No, I need some time to think, Alex. I'll catch you later."

It was just as well that Mor couldn't stay. Alex suddenly felt foolish worrying about the potter. He had no real reason to suspect the man was a murderer.

While he was waiting, Alex wanted to talk to Dave

Jeffries and see if they'd found any clues in the mass of spilled papers at the blacksmith's shop. Alex spoke to the dispatcher at the police station and asked, "Is Officer Jeffries around anywhere?"

The dispatcher said, "I'm sorry, he's on special assignment for the sheriff."

Alex sighed, then said, "Listen, when he gets back in, have him call Alex Winston at Hatteras West, would you?"

"I'll leave him a note, but I can't make any promises. He's probably going to be tied up all night."

Alex hung up the telephone, wondering what else he could do to help solve Jefferson Lee's murder. One thing was certain; there were questions he needed to ask Craig Monroe, and given the man's excitability, even if he hadn't killed the blacksmith, he could still be a dangerous man to back into a corner.

Alex didn't have a gun at the inn; he'd never seen any need for one. He did have several classic blunt instruments, though, and he placed the fireplace poker within reach of his favorite chair. Alex decided to light a fire and settle in for the wait.

He was still staring at the burning logs in the hearth when he heard the front door open. Craig Monroe came in, looking carefully around as he did.

"It's awfully quiet here," he said. "I didn't see a single car in the parking lot."

Alex lied, "I've got a guest upstairs, a hiker who walked in from town. He's a big brute," Alex added as he moved closer to the poker.

"I won't take long," Craig said as he slumped onto the couch opposite Alex. "This day has completely wiped me out."

"Any word on your wife?"

"No, she's still unconscious. The doctors won't call it a coma for some reason, but that's sure as hell what it looks like to me. She just lies there, hour after hour. I couldn't take it anymore."

Alex decided to end the suspense, one way or the other. "So what is it that's so urgent, Craig?"

"It's about Marilynn," Craig said. His words coming out in a rush, he continued, "We've been having problems lately. She was unfaithful. That's why this happened."

Was he confessing? "You must have been shattered when you found out."

Craig started pacing heavily around the room. Alex tried to keep his eyes on the man all the time, but it was like tracking a hummingbird.

Craig said, "You cannot imagine how furious I was. I still am, if you want to know the truth. That's not the worst part, though. I've got to tell somebody this, it's eating me up inside."

Alex started edging toward the poker. He only hoped he'd be quick enough to use it to defend himself.

Craig was nearly behind him when he said, "Alex, the worst part of this whole mess was the man she was cheating on me with." His voice suddenly turned icy cold. "My wife was having an affair with Jefferson Lee."

So that was Craig's motive; he was a betrayed husband! Alex was suddenly sure that Craig had him in his sights, but why? Alex hadn't seen or heard anything. Forget about subtlety, it was time to protect himself.

Alex started to pick up the poker just as Craig said, "Alex, I love Marilynn more than life itself. She felt so guilty cheating on me that she tried to kill herself. The only other possibility is that she couldn't bear to live anymore when her lover was murdered! Either way, it's all my fault, every bit of it. If I'd just showed her a little more attention . . . Alex, that's why her last words are so important to me. I have to know, was she thinking of Jefferson Lee when she did this to herself, or was she worried about me?"

The man's words choked off as he collapsed against Alex's chair, sobbing uncontrollably. Through the tears, he cried out, "What am I going to do if anything happens to her? She's my life!"

Alex dropped the poker and patted Craig's shoulder. "She's going to make it, you've got to have faith."

"Alex, I swear to you, if she does, I'm a changed man. I won't ever ignore her again. It nearly ripped my heart out when I found out she'd cheated on me, but this is destroying me."

There was nothing Alex could say.

After the tears ended, Craig looked spent. "I'm sorry, I don't know what happened to me just now."

"You're under a lot of stress. Why don't you go up to your old room and try to take a nap? You need to rest."

The man obviously felt awkward having Alex witness his breakdown. "No, I've got to get back to the hospital. The main reason I came out here was to see if Marilynn said anything at all when you found her."

"I'm sorry, but she was out of it by the time I got to her. What were you hoping for?"

He nearly whispered his answer. "I was praying she might have said she loved me." As the tears started flowing again, Craig hurried for the door. "I've got to get back."

Alex hated himself for thinking it, but he had to

wonder if Craig's outburst had been spontaneous and sincere, or if he'd been trying to throw Alex off his trail. If that were the case, though, why would he admit that his wife was having an affair with the murder victim? It could only hurt him, giving him a motive where none was known before. Unless he was leaking the information to Alex before he knew the police would find out, painting himself as a wronged man instead of a cold-blooded killer.

Alex was still twisting the possibilities over in his mind when the phone rang.

It was Elise.

"Hi, stranger," he said. "Any news?"

"Dad's complaining about the hospital bed and the food. It's the best sign we've had yet."

"I'm, glad," Alex said absently.

"Alex, is there something wrong?"

He sighed. "You just caught me at a bad time. There's a lot going on here."

"What's been happening?" she asked.

At that moment, Dave Jeffries came in. He saw Alex was on the phone, then tapped his watch.

"Listen, Elise, could I call you right back? Someone just came in I really need to talk to."

He could hear her stifle a yawn. "I'm going straight to bed, Alex. I'll talk to you tomorrow. Good night."

" 'Bye," he replied.

As he was hanging up, the deputy said, "Sorry to interrupt, Alex, but I'm on the clock. I got your message. What's up?"

"I just found out something the sheriff should know. Marilynn Baxter was having an affair with Jefferson Lee."

Dave clouded up. "Alex, tell me exactly what you

did at Lee's shop. You didn't take any letters with you, did you?"

"What are you talking about? I told you I didn't touch a thing."

Dave pressed him. "So how did you find out about the affair?"

"Craig Monroe just told me. I thought you should know he had a motive. Why are you so edgy all of a sudden?" Alex asked.

"That was my special assignment. After you left, I started digging around in the shop, and I found a secret cubby with letters from Marilynn to Jefferson Lee. They were pretty steamy. I figured one of them must have fallen out, and you were holding out on me. Sorry I jumped down your throat."

"So, do you think the killer was looking for those letters, or did Jefferson Lee have something else going on?"

"I truly don't know, Alex. Right now, I'm wondering if Craig didn't tell you first to take some of the sting out of us finding those letters. How was he when you talked to him?"

After a pause, Alex said, "He seemed genuinely upset about Marilynn's attempted suicide, but I couldn't say whether he killed Jefferson Lee or not."

"Don't worry, we'll nail him if he did." Dave looked at his watch. "Well, I can't hang around here all night. I've got to get back to Lee's shop and finish up. If you uncover anything else, call the sheriff. If you can't find him, call me, and I'll tell him myself."

"Thanks, Dave."

"Hey, we serve and protect, remember? Talk to you later, Alex."

After the deputy was gone, Alex dead-bolted the

inn's front door. It was rare that he could do it, since Alex couldn't lock his guests out, but he was glad for once that he was alone at Hatteras West.

Just in case, though, he dead-bolted the door to his room, too.

19

Alex felt a little silly the next morning unbolting all the locks. What did he think, Jefferson Lee's killer would come for him in the middle of the night? In the fresh light of a new day, Alex knew that the killer would have no reason to come after him. He was the first to admit that his unofficial investigation into the murder had produced very few results.

Alex was just going for his morning walk to the mailbox when Jenny Harris pulled up in her pickup truck. It wasn't all that unusual to find a woman who preferred trucks in the South. Jenny had more reason than most to have one; it was most likely the only way she could haul her heavy maple loom around wherever she went.

She rolled down the window as Alex approached. "Out for your morning constitutional?"

"Just getting the mail. What brings you back to Hatteras West?"

"I think something may have fallen out of my bag

while I was packing. I was hoping it might still be up in the room."

"You're welcome to come up to the inn and look around."

"Why don't you collect your mail, and I'll give you a ride back? It'll give us a chance to talk."

Alex said, "I appreciate the offer, but I really need the exercise. Tell you what. The rooms are all unlocked. Why don't you go up and check it out. I won't be long."

"Sounds good," she said as she drove the rest of the way to the inn. Alex wasn't being antisocial; the walk was one of his favorite parts of the day, a chance to be alone with his thoughts for the twenty minutes it took him to stroll to the box and back. In his busiest days of the year, it was the only time he truly had to himself. Elise had offered to walk with him at first, but he'd kept making excuses, and she'd finally stopped asking. It was his time, and he guarded it closely.

After he collected the mail, Alex walked back to the inn, glancing up at the lighthouse as he sorted through his mail. It was mostly bills, a few welcome deposit checks and a ton of junk mail.

Jenny was just coming out of his office when he walked inside. "I was just going to leave you a note. I thought you were never coming back."

"Have any luck?" he asked as he put the mail down on the front desk.

"No, I'm not sure where it's gone. So, have you heard anything about Jefferson's murder? I can't believe our esteemed sheriff let Bill Yadkin go."

"You sound positive he did it," Alex said.

"Well, when you take into account how much he hated Jefferson, his horrid temper and the murder weapon itself, I don't see how it could be anybody else."

Alex could think of at least three other people who could have committed the crime, but he kept the names to himself. "Did you hear about Marilynn Baxter?"

Jenny nodded her head sadly as she said, "I'm surprised it took her that long to try."

"Did I miss something?"

"Yes, but it's not your fault. Alex, there's a fair circuit some of us go on; it's the only way to pay the bills. It's mostly weekends, little fairs like this one where we have a chance to sell our wares and demonstrate our crafts. It's kind of a vagabond lifestyle, and we get to know each other pretty well. Almost too well, if you ask me. I've been waiting for Marilynn to snap. She's been fooling around behind Craig's back for months."

"How did you feel when you found out she was sleeping with Jefferson Lee?"

Jenny dismissed his statement with the wave of a hand. "It didn't happen while we were dating. Jefferson must have gone after Marilynn right after I dumped him. There just wasn't any real spark between us." She inhaled sharply, then suddenly said, "Oh my God."

Jenny had suddenly gone white.

Alex asked urgently, "What is it?"

"I just figured out why she tried to kill herself. I wonder if she killed Jefferson herself! That would explain why she took those pills. She couldn't face going to prison for the rest of her life."

"Slow down, Jenny. Do you have any proof that Marilynn killed him? What possible reason would she have for murdering him, especially the way it was done?"

"Don't be such a man, Alex. She killed him to save

her marriage. You know she's powerful enough to do it, working with her hands like she does. I don't doubt for one minute when she tried to end the affair, Jefferson told her he'd tell Craig what they'd been doing if she stopped seeing him. There's no doubt in my mind he would have used every bit of leverage he had. Suddenly it all makes sense."

Alex said, "Jenny, don't spread that rumor around town. Marilynn's got enough problems as it is at the moment."

"You're right, Alex. It's all sheer speculation, anyway." She glanced at the clock above the desk. "I can't believe the time. I'm late! Gotta run."

Jenny had been gone less than a minute when the telephone rang. "Alex, have you heard the news?"

It was Rachel, and she sounded upset.

Alex asked, "What's happened, Rachel?"

"Marilynn Baxter's dead."

Alex felt his heart sink at the news. He couldn't believe she was gone! Since he'd been the one to find her, Alex had been pulling for her to make it with all his heart.

"When did she die?" Alex asked sadly.

"Less than twenty minutes ago. Craig called and asked me to sit with her while he came out to see you, and I couldn't just leave the man alone when he got back. He was so distraught."

Alex could believe that. He'd had a feeling in his gut that Marilynn was going to pull through. He couldn't imagine what her husband was going through. "How's Craig taking it?"

"He's under sedation right now. They had a horrible time getting him away from the body."

"I can only imagine," Alex said. "Thanks for calling, Rachel."

Alex immediately phoned Doc Drake. When he was finally put through, he said, "Doc, I just heard about Marilynn Baxter."

"Yes, it was a real shame, Alex," the doctor said brusquely.

"Excuse me for saying so, but you don't sound all that upset about it."

Doc took a deep breath, then said, "Alex, I've been up all night with two different emergencies, both of my patients fighting for their lives with every ounce of strength left in them. Marilynn Baxter threw her life away by choice. I'm sorry, it might sound heartless to you, but I don't have any tears left for her. I'll save my emotions for the ones fighting for their last chance."

In all the years he'd known Doc Drake, Alex had never heard him sound so cynical. "I'm sorry. I was just concerned. To be honest with you, I sort of felt like I had a stake in her well-being, since I'm the one who found her."

Doc took a deep breath, then said, "Alex, I'm the one who's sorry. I've been up around the clock, and I still have a full day of work staring at me. I'm sorry for what I said. I hate losing *any* of my patients, you know that. Now, if you'll excuse me, I'm going to take a nap. I have seventeen minutes before my first patient, and I plan to sleep sixteen of them."

Alex wondered what Craig Monroe would be like now that his wife was dead. Alex remembered the shivers Craig had given him the night before, and though he felt foolish about his reactions in the light of day, he couldn't help wondering if his instincts were trying to tell him something. Was Craig Monroe a grieving spouse, or was he a murderer, intent on covering the last vestiges of his trail? More importantly, did Monroe believe that Alex had held back on him, refusing to share something damning his wife had said? He'd believed Craig when the man had broken down, but could it all have been an act? Alex was going to have to watch his step until he knew for sure.

Alex found himself with time weighing heavily on his hands at The Hatteras West. With no guests at the inn, he'd easily done his day's work in the morning, and while he liked someone to always be at the front desk to answer the phone, he was going crazy all by himself. The travel agent had called with regrets, so that was that. There was really no other reason to hang around. Finally, Alex decided to hang a sign out front and lock the place up tight. He believed in his heart that the answers he was looking for were in town, not at Hatteras West.

The first place Alex stopped was at Shantara's General Store. Alex loved the old mercantile; he had since he was a kid, though his friend hadn't owned it then. Old Mr. Gruber had been delighted to have kids explore the shelves filled with treasures every inch of the way. Shantara hadn't changed much of the old, but she'd added enough new to give the place her own mark. The tiny post office was still in one corner, with its odd little boxes and the iron-barred window in front of it. The aisles held everything from massive electric coolers stocked with chilled beverages to shelves filled with nails, screws, kitchen gadgets and a thousand other things a general store should have.

The shelves on the outside walls featured biscuit mixes, pots, pans and all types of specialty goods that weren't available anywhere else in town. Shantara had added a craft corner where the old pickle barrel had once stood, displaying samples from many of the people who had worked the Golden Days Fair. Another corner featured a potbellied stove with three mismatched rocking chairs around it, while the fourth corner held the sales counter and the cash register, a machine that looked old-fashioned but in fact was a modern piece of equipment.

Alex found Shantara behind the counter selling Jake Trush a pound of sixteen-penny nails.

"I should have bought an inn instead of a farm," Jake said, smiling when he saw Alex. "It must be nice goofing off in the middle of the day."

Alex knew the man was just trying to be neighborly, but he wasn't in the mood for light banter. Still, he had to hold up his end of the exchange, or the word would go out that Alex was in a "bad way," no doubt attributed to Elise's absence.

He said as lightly as he could manage, "Yeah, it probably is nice not to be working, but I wouldn't know a thing about it. If I find somebody who *is* goofing off, I'll be sure to give him a pat on the back."

Jake smiled. "Give him a rap for me, too, will you? See you later, Shantara. You know what they say: Every new project takes three trips to the store before it's done."

"You've got one more coming then, Jake."

After he was gone, Shantara said, "What brings you over here in the middle of the day, Alex? Not that I'm not glad for your company."

"I thought you might like to know. Marilynn Baxter just died."

"I found out an hour ago. Alex, from what I've heard, she never really had a chance."

"Is there anything you don't know, Shantara?"

"It's part and parcel to running a general store. Everybody and his brother shows up sooner or later, and it's a rare customer who doesn't have a bit of gossip to share over this counter." Shantara lowered her voice as she added, "I just wish I knew who killed Jefferson Lee. Alex, I won't feel safe until they arrest someone."

"Have you heard anything at all about that?"

Shantara shook her head. "Nobody's talking. Dave Jeffries came by when he got off work, but all I could get out of him was that they were still following leads. I got the impression the sheriff was about to arrest Bill Yadkin, though."

"I know. Rachel's worried sick about it." Alex was about to tell Shantara his suspicions about the other suspects on his list when a young woman came in with three overactive kids.

"Sorry, Alex, I can't really talk right now."

"I'll see you later." As Alex left the store, he headed for Buck's Grill on foot.

Even if he didn't make any progress in his investigation, at least he'd get something to eat.

20

"Alex, are you following me?"

He was approaching the counter at Buck's Grill when he heard Sandra's voice coming from one of the nearby booths.

"No, I just dropped in for a quick bite."

Alex was just about to slide onto a stool when she said, "I just got here myself. Why don't you join me?" Sandra lowered her voice as she added, "You can pay for your own meal, I promise."

Alex wasn't all that fond of eating by himself either, though he'd grown more or less used to it over the years before Elise came onto the scene. He slid into the booth and noticed Sally Anne's eyebrows shoot up when she saw him hesitate at the counter before joining his ex-girlfriend.

She stopped at the table, sliding a glass of iced tea in front of Alex. "The usual?"

"Sounds good to me."

After Sally Anne left to deliver the order to her father, Sandra said, "So, you still have your standing order here. Some things never change, Alex."

"And some things do," he replied.

"Hi, Alex," Jenny Harris said brightly as she stopped by their table on her way out the door. "If I'd known you were coming here later, we could have had lunch together."

Sandra said, "Sorry, Jenny, but he's already got a lunch date."

Jenny smiled as she said, "I sincerely doubt that."

"Easy, ladies, I'm not on a date with anyone. Jenny, Sandra and I just ran into each other, it's that simple. You're more than welcome to join us if you'd like."

"No thanks, I'm on my way out," Jenny said as she twisted her purse strap in her hands. She smiled as she added, "Besides, it would probably look like a meeting of the Alex Winston Ex-girlfriends' Club."

"We'd need a bigger booth than this one," Sandra said with a laugh.

Jenny headed out the door after paying her bill, and Smiley O'Reilly stopped by the table a second later. "Sorry about your loss."

"What are talking about, Smiley?"

"Heard your maid quit for good. Too bad."

Before Alex could say a word, Smiley was gone.

Sandra hesitated a moment after the insurance man left, then said, "You look like you just lost your best friend."

Alex said, "I'm just tired of everyone around town assuming Elise isn't coming back to Elkton Falls." He took a sip of tea, then added, "I guess maybe a part of me is afraid they're right."

Sandra reached a hand across the table and touched Alex's arm lightly. "Whether she comes back or not, it's no fault of yours, Alex. Maybe life in Elkton Falls isn't everything she'd hoped it would be. Not everyone's cut out for small-town living, you know."

Alex said, "You know, now that you mention it, I'm surprised you came back home after college, Sandra."

She tilted her head askance. "What, and give up the fine cuisine offered here?"

"Seriously. Why did you come back?"

Sandra drank some of the tea in front of her, studying the surface as if she could read the future in it. Finally, she said, "I guess I like being a big fish in a small pond. There's not a lot of competition for me here, and I get most of the best cases. I like being able to see a dozen people I know every day, no matter where I go. I like the history of the place. The foothills and mountains are in my blood, Alex, and I can't think of anyplace in the world prettier than it is right here. I guess what it boils down to is, this is home."

Her last three words summed up all of Alex's own reasons for staying in Elkton Falls. The lighthouse, the Keeper's Quarters, Bear Rocks; he couldn't imagine living without them as a constant and reassuring presence in his life.

"You're awfully quiet," Sandra said. "I didn't mean to bring you down even more."

"You didn't," Alex said, trying to lighten his mood. He saw Emma Sturbridge coming toward them from one of the back booths. Alex knew too well what had caused the grim look on Emma's face as she neared their table. The clouds had to be lingering from her earlier time with Mor.

Emma suddenly tried to brighten her demeanor as she said loudly, "Why, Alex, how are you?"

As if they hadn't just seen each other yesterday.

"I'm fine, Emma. And you?"

She ignored the question. "Have you heard from Elise lately?"

"We spoke for a few minutes last night," Alex admitted.

As she gave Sandra a sideways glance, Emma broadcast, "Elise Danton is a fine woman. I can't wait till she gets back to Elkton Falls. I expect it to be anytime, don't you? I'm sure you've missed her sorely at the inn." Emma reached over and patted his shoulder. "Now don't you worry about a thing. She asked me personally to help out until she comes back, and I promise you, I'll be there for you. I'm certain she'll be back any day."

Mor, having paid the check, joined them. "Come on, Emma, lower your voice. Half the town can hear you."

Emma shot him a stern glance. "Are you ready to go, Mor? I believe we still have a few more issues to discuss."

The big man nodded his agreement. "You're right about that. See you later Alex, Sandra."

After they were gone, Sandra said, "Elise certainly has a good friend in that woman."

"It's true; they hit it off from the very start."

Sandra shook her head; there was a faint smile on her lips. "Alex, that speech was aimed a great deal more in my direction than yours. Emma wanted to make certain that I knew your maid was coming back and not to get too cozy in the seat across from you."

"How do you get all that from what she just said?" Alex asked.

Sandra was saved an answer by the arrival of their food. She managed to steer their conversation in a thousand directions, all of them directly away from Elise Danton.

After they'd eaten, Alex said, "Sandra, I need to ask

you something. Do you really think Armstrong's going to arrest Bill Yadkin for the murder?"

Sandra said, "I gave up trying to figure our sheriff out long ago." She lowered her voice as she added, "I shouldn't say this, but it wouldn't surprise me in the least. I'm afraid Bill's temper is going to be his downfall." As she pulled her check from the two on the table, Sandra said, "Alex, I don't know how well you two know each other, but he needs every friend he's got right now."

She stood beside the table, and before walking to the register, Sandra added, "Alex, for your sake, I do hope Elise comes back soon. I really mean it. I know how much you miss her."

"Thanks," Alex said, amazed that Sandra was being so adult about it all. After all, he'd been the one to break their relationship off, one of the reasons being so he could pursue something with Elise. Though that hadn't materialized, Alex knew the breakup had still hurt Sandra's feelings. As he paid his own check, Alex wondered if Sandra did indeed think Elise was gone for good.

It could be she was just being gracious in her victory.

Alex decided to take Sandra's advice and pop in on Bill Yadkin before heading back to the inn.

He heard angry voices coming from the shop in back of the man's house when he arrived. Calling it a shop was quite generous. The blacksmith's building was in stark contrast with the modern efficiency of Jefferson Lee's workplace. Bill's equipment could have been taken from a smithy a hundred years before, with massive leather bellows by his forge and a faded black anvil that looked ancient to Alex. No fire was burning in the forge, though. All of the heat was coming from Bill Yadkin as he argued with Rachel Seabock.

"I don't care. Do you hear me?" Bill shouted, the words dying as he spotted Alex behind him. "What do you want?"

"I thought you might need a friend about now," Alex said gently.

Rachel snapped, "Alex, you try pounding some sense into him, he won't listen to me."

Alex saw that the young blacksmith had a bag by his side, obviously full of clothes and some of his most precious tools. "Going somewhere, Bill?"

"I'm getting as far away from Elkton Falls as I can, if it's any of your business!"

Rachel snapped, "Bill! He just wants to help!"

Bill Yadkin threw a set of metal pincers down on his anvil so hard the steel rang. "That's the trouble with this place! Everybody just wants to help. Why don't you people get it through your thick skulls? I don't need any help!"

Alex said calmly, "The biggest mistake you can make in the world right now is running away. I'll wait until you finish your little tantrum before I tell you why." He pointed to a bucket of water beside the anvil. "Why don't you soak your head in that bucket for a while until you cool off?"

Alex fought the fear in him as the blacksmith's strong hands twisted a knot in the handle of his bag. There was a rage and an energy in the young blacksmith that was truly frightening, but Alex knew if he showed the slightest sign of weakness, it could spell disaster.

Rachel started to say something, then thought better of it and remained mute.

It took a few moments, but Bill's anger suddenly dissipated. "Yeah, maybe you're right. A good soaking might do me some good. So why shouldn't I leave before that knobby-kneed sheriff throws me in jail?"

"If you run, it's just going to look like you really did kill Jefferson Lee. There's a lot of anger in you, isn't there?"

"I've got a temper, I'm the first to admit it, but I'd never kill anyone. I swear it."

For some reason he couldn't fathom, Alex believed him. He knew he could easily be wrong, but his gut was telling him that the young blacksmith was telling the truth.

Rachel said, "Bill, don't you see that Alex is right? You can't run away from this. I'll stay by your side; you know it's true."

Yadkin put a powerful hand on her shoulder. "I know you will, Rachel. It's just so frustrating. Everybody in town thinks I'm a killer."

"Not everybody," Alex said. "You've got Rachel and me on your side."

Bill nodded. "I thank you for that, Alex. Maybe you're right."

Alex looked at him and grinned. "Maybe?"

Bill chuckled at that. "Okay, I admit it, you're right. Alex, I'm sorry I snapped at you. You didn't do a thing in the world to deserve it." He held out a meaty paw, and Alex took it. There was power to crush in that grip, but Bill's clasp stopped at a firm warmth.

"I guess I'd better unpack this stuff before Armstrong comes along and gets the wrong idea."

"I'll be inside in a second," Rachel said as Bill Yadkin headed back into his modest house.

"Alex, I don't know what I would have done if you hadn't come along when you did."

"I'm glad I could help." He looked back toward the house. "Is he going to be all right?"

"I think so. I've been trying to get him to think straight since all this mess started, but that's the first time I've seen the man I care about since Jefferson Lee's murder. Alex, do you really believe him? It's important that I know you're not just saying it to keep him in town."

"I'll be honest with you, Rachel, I couldn't give you a reason that would stand up in a court of law, but I do think he's telling the truth. I'm worried, though. If he doesn't get that temper under control, it could be bad news for him. I'm not trying to scare you, but you know it's the truth."

"I'm working on it, Alex. That's all I can do." She squeezed his hand lightly as she added, "Honestly, you men are so hard to train."

"Yes, but we're worth the effort, aren't we?" Alex said with a smile.

"Sometimes," Rachel admitted as she headed for the house.

Alex had gone around town searching for answers, but he hadn't learned anything new. Something was niggling at the back of his mind; the only problem was, he couldn't put his finger on what it was.

Alex wanted to talk to Shantara again.

Maybe chewing things over with his old friend would jar something loose.

At that point, it was the best he could hope for.

As Alex walked toward Shantara's store, he had the distinct feeling that someone was watching him. Trying to be cool, he looked over his shoulder, but he couldn't see a soul paying him any attention at all.

Chiding himself for his overactive imagination, Alex hurried his pace nevertheless.

21

"Hey, anybody here?" Alex called out as he walked into Shantara's store.

"I'm over here," she said, and Alex followed her voice to the craft corner. Shantara was trying to hang a large, woven shawl on a hanger from a high nail. The handwork was obviously one of Jenny's latest bright creations.

Alex said, "Let me help you with that."

She said haughtily, "Just because you're a man doesn't mean you can do something I can't, Alex Winston."

He plucked the hanger from Shantara's hands and eased it over the nail. "It's not because I'm a man; it's because I'm taller than you are."

She wrinkled her nose at him, then said with a smile, "Okay, maybe I overreacted. I'm still walking on eggshells around here, hoping nobody finds out my connection with Jefferson Lee." For once the store was empty, so Shantara had no reason to lower her voice.

Even Marcie was gone, no doubt enjoying some well-earned vacation time.

Alex asked, "Is that shawl new? I don't think I've seen it here before."

Shantara said, "Rachel had it on approval, but she didn't want it. Why, I'll never know, especially at the discount she gets."

"Why does she rate a discount on Jenny Harris's handwork?"

Shantara explained, "All of the crafters at the fair formed a little friendly circle long ago, even Jefferson Lee. They can buy each other's wares at half the retail price. I guess it's a way for them to support each other's work. Jenny told me last week she spent too much money this month at Bill Yadkin's shop, even with her discount. She's been hanging curtains in her house, and you should see the ironwork that girl has on display."

Shantara looked longingly at the shawl and said, "You know, it's ironic. I sell these things, but I can't afford them."

Alex said, "Why don't you treat yourself? You told me you made enough from the fair to more than get you out of the hole."

Shantara looked at the shawl and said, "Would you mind getting it back down?"

Alex retrieved the shawl and ceremoniously wrapped it around Shantara's shoulders. "I have to admit that it looks awfully good on you."

Shantara said, "Why, Alex, it's such a generous gift. You shouldn't have."

Alex laughed as he looked at the extravagant price printed heavily on the tag. "I didn't. Maybe I'd better go ahead and hang it back up."

She pulled away from him. "No, I think I'll take

your advice and buy this for myself." She winked as she added, "Maybe I can talk Jenny into extending her discount to me just this once. I make a profit on everything I sell for the crafters, but it's certainly not half."

Alex said, "I'm here for a reason besides your sunny presence. I want to ask you something."

"Fire away."

As Shantara moved to dust some of Marilynn and Craig's pottery on the shelf, Alex said; "I keep coming back to the reason Jefferson Lee was killed, and I can't understand something. You've been around these crafters longer than I have. Do you think Craig Monroe would kill Jefferson if he found out the man was having an affair with his wife?"

Shantara frowned, but she showed no shock from the news.

"So you know about that, too," Alex added gently.

"I'm afraid everyone in our little circle did. Craig confronted Jefferson right after he found out. I was there, along with the other crafters. It got ugly, but their confrontation never came to blows. Alex, to be honest with you, Craig Monroe would do a great many things to make Jefferson Lee's life miserable, but I can't imagine him killing him."

"Could you be wrong?" Alex asked.

"I could be, but I don't think so. I'm not saying he couldn't kill Jefferson, but he wouldn't use an iron skewer; he'd be more likely to attack the man with his fists, if you want my opinion. Did I say something wrong?" Shantara asked when she saw the frown on Alex's face.

"No, I had a thought, but now it's gone. Okay, if Jefferson wasn't killed for competition or love or money, why was he killed?"

"Just because you've ruled out a motive for one suspect doesn't mean you can't apply it to a different person. There was a lot Jefferson Lee was keeping close to the vest. I can't prove it, but there's no doubt in my mind that he had more than one girlfriend when he was murdered."

Suddenly it struck home, that elusive clue he'd been grasping for. That was the key Alex had been trying to get his hands on!

He enveloped Shantara in his arms and lifted her off the ground in a hug.

"What was that for?" she asked when he put her back down.

"You just gave me the last piece of the puzzle I needed. I know who murdered Jefferson Lee."

"Don't keep it to yourself. Who did it?"

Alex backed down from the strength of his earlier statement. "Knowing it is one thing. Proving it will be something else entirely."

"So tell me your suspicions. I don't mind a little idle gossip."

Alex shook his head. "Shantara, what if I'm wrong? I'm not going to smear a good name any more than I have to. I've got to dig a little deeper before I'm ready to share my theories with anyone else."

As he was leaving, Shantara called out, "Just don't dig too deeply, Alex. You don't want to end up digging your own grave."

As Alex left the shop, a thousand thoughts boiled over in his mind. Did he have enough evidence to go to the sheriff? Did he have any choice? What if his delay caused another murder?

No, he couldn't live with that.

Ready or not, Alex had to find the sheriff and tell him who the real murderer was, before they could strike again.

Alex searched all over Elkton Falls for Sheriff Armstrong. The dispatch office wasn't any help at all. The sheriff was off on two hours of personal time, and he couldn't be disturbed, even if Alex could get the dispatcher to admit knowing where Armstrong was.

Alex decided to ask for Dave Jeffries instead. After all, he knew Dave well enough to tell him his suspicions. Unfortunately, the deputy was out of the office and couldn't be reached, either. Alex wondered who was protecting the citizens of Elkton Falls if the sheriff and his best deputy were out of touch. He finally left a message requesting that the sheriff or the deputy come to Hatteras West as soon as they could get there. Until then, all Alex could do was wait.

Driving to the inn, Alex was glad to be heading back home. The Hatteras West was his harbor in a world gone mad, the only place he truly felt safe.

As Alex walked in through the front door, he saw Jenny Harris standing behind the desk going through his guest book.

As he tried to back out of the room, she held a gun up and said, "Come on, Alex. Things are just getting interesting. You don't want to leave now, do you?"

With a gun pointed at him, Alex gained little satisfaction in knowing that his suspicions had been right.

Alex said, "There's a part of me that still can't believe you killed Jefferson Lee. You had to be insane to get the strength to skewer him to the post like that."

Her voice was calm and reasonable as she explained, "You've obviously never wrestled a heavy maple weaving frame around. I'm a lot stronger than you could ever imagine, Alex."

"What about the murder weapon? *Was* it one of Bill Yadkin's pieces?"

"Hardly. The swooping design on the end of the

shaft was easy enough for Jefferson to duplicate. He'd done it as one final favor if I promised to leave him alone after that. I told him it had to match a set Bill had made, and that his younger competition had claimed Jefferson didn't have the skill to match it. It was that simple. How delightful I ended up using it on him."

"What about the postcard I found in Jefferson's room? That was from you, wasn't it? I saw how heavily you pressed down on the pen when you wrote it, then I saw the same thing on one of your price tags at Shantara's store."

Jenny's voice was filled with disdain. "Of course it was from me. When I found you'd made copies of it, I knew you were on my trail. What happened to the original?"

"I took it back upstairs, and the sheriff found it."

She shook her head. "I was never worried about him figuring this out. You've been my main threat all along, Alex. I suppose you found my bracelet in your office."

He nodded. "At first I thought Elise had dropped it, but the more I played with it, the more certain I was that it belonged to someone else. I knew I'd seen it before, but I just remembered an hour ago that it was on your wrist, not Elise's. You wore it the first day of the fair as you worked at your loom."

"I came back here to look for it, and when I found it in your room, I knew it was only a matter of time until you figured it out." As Jenny's finger tightened on the trigger, she added, "I'm sorry it had to end this way, but you really didn't leave me any choice."

22

"Don't do anything stupid, Jenny. You can't get away with this."

She smiled softly as she brought the gun up toward Alex's chest. Jenny was ten feet away from him; there was no way she could miss at that range.

She said sadly, "Alex, you're my last loose thread. Once I take care of you, there won't be any trail leading back to me. I'm sorry. I really did like you, Alex."

Alex scanned the lobby, trying to come up with anything he could use to defend himself. He was too close to the wall to be within reach of the fireplace poker.

So what could he use? The closest thing to him was the end table with the ornate iron piece Jefferson Lee had made perched on the edge of it. Alex couldn't imagine using it as a weapon, but what choice did he have? If he could distract Jenny by throwing the iron at her, maybe he could get outside. No one knew the land around Hatteras West better than he did, and if Alex could just manage to escape out the front door, he might still have a fighting chance.

It had to be better than just standing there, waiting for Jenny Harris to pull the trigger.

Before Alex could make his move, he had to divert her attention.

Alex prodded her. "How did you manage to kidnap Marilynn? Why did you kill her, Jenny? I can't imagine that she really committed suicide."

Jenny laughed softly. "Alex, you're giving me way too much credit. I had nothing to do with her disappearance or her death. I imagine she was feeling so wracked with guilt over betraying her husband that she overdosed." A slight frown crossed Jenny's face. "I admit I thought about getting rid of her at one point, but I'm not an animal, Alex. Jefferson deserved to die. He dumped me the second he thought I was pregnant! The irony was, it was nothing but a false alarm. When I tried to tell him, he laughed at me! Can you imagine how I felt? I had the staff in my hands, he'd just finished it at the fair. What choice did Jefferson leave me? It was his own fault. I wasn't going to stand there and take his derision, Alex! He deserved exactly what he got!"

It was now or never. Alex reached around in one swift motion, plucked the ironwork off the table and hurled it toward Jenny just as she fired. He felt a sting bite one arm as he threw the ironwork, but he couldn't afford to see how badly he'd been hit until he was someplace safe.

Alex made it to the door just as another bullet thunked into the wood frame beside him with a meaty slap.

She was good, too good for his tastes!

Alex ran away from the lighthouse the second he was out the door; it had been a benevolent presence for him all his life, but the sentinel was nothing but a deadly trap for him at the moment.

Suddenly, Alex knew exactly where to go: Bear Rocks. If he could get into the maze of stones first, she'd never find him. Sooner or later, Armstrong would get his message and be out there.

He only hoped the sheriff would make it in time.

"Alex, you can't run away from me," he heard Jenny call as he dove into the copse of trees between the inn and Bear Rocks. Alex ran in a zigzag pattern, trying to throw her aim off, but it appeared Jenny was saving her bullets. He glanced back to see how far away she was just before he dove down the first rock slide.

She was close, and Alex saw with satisfaction that the ironwork he'd thrown had struck home. Jenny was bleeding steadily above one eye. Instead of slowing her down though, it looked as if it had only served to make her even more determined to kill him.

"You can't escape, Alex. Why make it more painful than it has to be?"

If he could get her lost in the rocks, he might even be able to get away. There was a highway on the other side of the rock formation that led back into town. With any luck, he could cover the distance that stood between before she even realized he wasn't in the rocks anymore.

"There you are," he heard her say close behind him. A bullet suddenly zinged off a rock two inches from his right hand! She'd climbed to Cradle Rock and was using it to look down on him.

Alex dove down, twisting and turning his adult body through passageways that had been spacious when he'd been a kid but had grown claustrophobic in the interim. He knew he was bruising and scraping his body as he hurried, but Alex forced the minor pains out of his mind, though his arm throbbed violently every time he brushed it against another rock.

Alex could deal with the pain. He had to. At the moment, he had one task, and that was to escape with his life.

His foot stumbled on loose rock, and he almost went down with a twisted ankle. Fortunately, he caught himself before he fell, though the jarring contact with the stone sent another wave of nausea through him.

The loose gravel gave him an idea. Alex had been a pretty decent pitcher in high school, though he hadn't thrown much since. Maybe, just maybe, he could clip her shooting hand and make her drop the gun. At least she'd shot him in the right arm; he thanked the stars above that he was left-handed.

"Come out, come out wherever you are," Jenny called, laughing.

Alex stuck his head up quickly and saw her back was to him now. He'd managed to work his way around her! Taking a stone the size of a softball, Alex hurled it at her head. It struck her shoulder instead, nearly spinning her around with its impact.

When she faced him again, there was a look of pure hatred on her face. She was almost unrecognizable.

Alex heard the shot whistle past his ear as he ducked down again.

After she realized she'd missed, Jenny said, "Now Alex, why did you have to do that? It's going to leave a bruise for weeks! I'm afraid I'll have to punish you for being bad. Come out like a good boy and take what you've got coming." There was a cloying edge to her tone that set his teeth on edge.

He had to get another clear shot at her. Rushing through a precarious passageway he hadn't been through in twenty-five years, Alex moved quickly among the rocks.

When he looked back at her, Alex saw that she'd been moving in the same general direction! She was much too close! He'd have to throw the stone in his hand and get back down before it hit. Zipping it toward her, she must have sensed something, because Jenny whirled around, sending a wild shot screaming into the rocks above him. Her aim was definitely getting worse.

Alex couldn't afford to see if the stone had struck home.

Hurrying down another passageway, he kept moving until he was sure he was far enough away to throw another stone.

He was wrong.

There, standing less than a foot away from him, Jenny had her revolver trained straight at Alex's head.

There was no way out.

Alex's time had just run out.

"Jenny, let's talk about this," Alex said, trying to figure a way out of the jam he was in now.

"Enough talking," she shrieked. "Now it's time to die. Alex, I'm truly sorry. I really did like you."

"Hold it right there."

Alex looked over his shoulder to see Sheriff Armstrong twenty feet away. He had his gun drawn, and there was a look of steel in his gaze that Alex had never seen before.

Jenny snapped, "Put that away, you idiot. If you shoot me, I'll kill him before I die. There's no way you can stop me."

Alex said, "Jenny, what good will that do? You're going to be caught; there's no escape now."

She said snappishly, "I've already killed one man,

Alex. What are they going to do, execute me again for killing you? What have I got to lose?"

Alex said softly, "Flip the coin, Jenny. What have you got to gain?"

"Are you kidding me? You toyed with me one too many times. You have to pay for that, Alex."

He touched his arm and pulled away a bloody palm. As he held it out to her, he said, "Don't you think I've paid enough?"

"Oh, that's just the start of it, Alex." There was a look of pure, intense hatred on her face as she said it.

Then she pulled the trigger.

Alex kept waiting for the explosion of pain that never came. Jenny cursed the gun, trying to figure out why it hadn't fired, but Alex didn't hesitate. He threw the last of his rocks at her, then climbed toward her just as she hurled the gun at his head.

It missed, clattering off the rocks behind him.

"Enough," Armstrong roared. "If you don't freeze this instant, you're going to die!"

"So shoot me," Jenny screamed. "I don't care!"

"Stop," Alex shouted as he fought to scale the rocks between them. She was still cursing as he wrapped his arms around Jenny in a bearlike grip so she couldn't move. "Don't shoot, Sheriff. I've got her."

It was an awkward embrace, but Jenny couldn't escape, that was what was important. Instead, when she realized that she wasn't going anywhere but jail, she buried her face in Alex's chest, sobbing. "He had to die, Alex, he had to. Don't you see? He had to die."

Alex wanted to feel pity for her, but he couldn't. All he could see was Jefferson Lee's lifeless body pinned against the beam with a steel shaft through his heart.

Jenny gave up completely. She was surprisingly docile as Armstrong put the cuffs on her. After the sheriff put her in the back of the squad car, Armstrong said, "Sorry I couldn't get here sooner, Alex. I was taking care of some personal business, and I didn't get your message until it was almost too late."

"Don't beat yourself up over it. Everything worked out fine, Sheriff."

Armstrong looked at Alex's arm. "You'd better get that checked out pretty quick. Why don't you ride into town with me?"

The last thing in the world Alex wanted to do was to spend another second in Jenny Harris's company.

He was spared that, at least.

A voice behind him said, "That won't be necessary, Sheriff. I'll see that he gets there."

Alex couldn't believe it. Elise was standing a few feet away, a worried look on her face.

She'd come back to Hatteras West after all.

23

"Oomph," Alex grunted as Elise accidentally brushed against him. The pain in his right arm was really intensifying now that his adrenaline rush was nearly over. Waves of angry bolts shot through him every time he so much as moved.

"Oh, Alex, I hurt you! I'm so sorry."

"It's not that bad," he said. "I'm so glad you're back, Elise."

She frowned gently. "I wouldn't leave for good, Alex, you should know that. This place is too important to me. Listen, we can talk about that later. Right now, we need to get you to the hospital."

"Okay," he agreed as he fished his keys out of his pocket. "You'd better drive, though."

"Alex, I've missed you," she said calmly as she helped him into the passenger seat of his truck.

"I've missed you, too. How's your dad?"

As Elise drove, she said, "He's good enough to go

back to the inn and recuperate there. I stayed as long as I was needed, but it just wasn't the same anymore."

"Sometimes I imagine it's tough going home again," Alex said.

"That's the whole problem, Alex. It wasn't home. Elkton Falls is my home now."

It was the best thing in the world she could have said to him.

Doc Drake was at the emergency room, having just taken care of young Jimmy Hickman's broken arm.

As he worked on cleaning Alex's wound, he said, "You are the luckiest man I know. The bullet just grazed you, Alex. I'll be able to stitch you up and have you out of here in no time. I never would have believed Jenny Harris would snap like that."

"If you'd seen what I had, you'd believe it easily enough."

As he finished bandaging the wound, Doc said, "Well, you've been through a lot today. You need anything to help you sleep tonight?"

"No, I'll be fine," Alex said.

Doc Drake grinned. "I hear someone's waiting for you outside. You'd better not keep her standing there in the hallway much longer."

Alex offered his left hand to the doctor to shake.

When the door suddenly opened, Alex expected to see Elise, but he found Sheriff Armstrong instead.

"Got a second, Alex?"

"Just about that. I need to get home, Sheriff."

Doc Drake said, "If you two will excuse me, I've got another patient to see."

After the doctor was gone, Armstrong said, "I just

wanted to let you know what I found out." He gestured to Alex's arm. "I figure I owe you that."

"It wasn't your fault I got shot."

Armstrong hung his head. "Nice of you to say so, but I can't say I'd agree with it. I shouldn't have been so bent on pinning the murder on Yadkin. I made a mistake there, one I won't likely repeat."

"It's okay," Alex said.

Armstrong nodded, then said, "I just found out where Marilynn Baxter was hiding out. Her neighbor Ruby Garnet came into the station an hour ago and told me she'd been helping Marilynn lie low. Ruby feels something awful about letting her go back alone when she was still so distraught, but she couldn't have known."

"The only thing she's guilty of is having a big heart," Alex agreed.

Armstrong said, "On the way to the station, I asked Jenny about breaking into Jefferson Lee's shop. Seems Jefferson had himself a Polaroid Camera, and he liked to use it when they were, uh, you know, together. Jenny said she found the pictures and burned them before she came after you. She kept saying you were her last loose thread. You're lucky to be alive, Alex."

"Don't I know it," Alex said as he got up, holding his arm gently. "Thanks for the update, Sheriff, I truly do appreciate it, but I really need to go home."

Armstrong made a motion to pat Alex's shoulder but stopped abruptly. "I'll be out at the inn later to check on Irene. She's working the crime scene."

Alex almost tripped over Elise as he opened the door to leave.

"Alex, I was so worried about you. Are you all right?"

He lifted the sutured arm gently in the air. "I'm just

glad I'm left-handed, or I would have never been able to throw those rocks at Jenny. I think that's what saved my life."

"I'm so sorry I wasn't there for you, Alex. You needed me, and I let you down."

As they walked toward the clerk's desk to settle his bill, Alex said, "You had to go back for your father, Elise. You don't owe me any apologies."

"Well, I'm here now." She paused, then asked, "What's going on with Mor and Emma? They were out in the waiting room with me, then all of a sudden they started arguing about something in whispers. The next thing I knew, they both just got up and left."

"They've been trying to iron out the differences in their relationship over the past couple of days. I think they're either going to break up after all this is over or get engaged."

Elise said, "Which one are you pulling for?"

Alex sighed. "That one's easy. Whichever solution makes my friends the happiest."

Elise nodded. "Well said. Alex, why don't we get you back to the inn, and I'll fix you a nice dinner. How does that sound?"

"That's the best offer I've had all day." He knew Hatteras West's lobby would still be in the middle of Irene's crime scene investigation, but he didn't care.

All Alex really wanted to do was to go home. He drew energy from the lighthouse, from Bear Rocks, from all of The Hatteras West Inn.

Having Elise there with him again was more than he could ever ask for.

It was time to go home.

About the Author

Tim Myers lives with his family near the Blue Ridge Mountains he loves and writes about. He is the award-winning author of over seventy short stories. Mr. Myers has been a stay-at-home dad for the last ten years, finding time for murder and mayhem whenever he can.

To learn more, visit his website at **www.timmyers.net** or contact him at **timothylmyers@hotmail.com**.

Penguin Putnam Inc.
Online

Your Internet gateway to a virtual environment with
hundreds of entertaining and enlightening books
from Penguin Putnam Inc.

*While you're there, get the latest buzz on
the best authors and books around—*

Tom Clancy, Patricia Cornwell, W.E.B. Griffin,
Nora Roberts, William Gibson, Robin Cook,
Brian Jacques, Catherine Coulter, Stephen King,
Jacquelyn Mitchard, and many more!

**Penguin Putnam Online is located at
http://www.penguinputnam.com**

PENGUIN PUTNAM NEWS

Every month you'll get an inside look at our upcoming books and new features on our site. This is an
ongoing effort to provide you with the most
up-to-date information about
our books and authors.

**Subscribe to Penguin Putnam News at
http://www.penguinputnam.com/ClubPPI**